Sarah's Long Ride

Sarah's Long Ride
SUSAN PAGE DAVIS

Greenville, South Carolina

Library of Congress Cataloging-in-Publication Data

Davis, Susan Page.
  Sarah's long ride / by Susan Page Davis.
     p. cm.
  Summary: When newly orphaned Sarah goes to live with her
quiet Uncle Joe on his isolated Oregon ranch, she prays that he
will allow her to continue the trail riding competitions she and her
mother had loved so much, and that the two of them will learn to
feel like a family.
  ISBN 978-1-59166-737-7 (perfect bound pbk. : alk. paper)
  [1. Horses—Fiction. 2. Uncles—Fiction. 3. Ranch life—
Oregon—Fiction. 4. Orphans—Fiction. 5. Christian life—Fiction.
6. Oregon—Fiction.] I. Title.
  PZ7.D3172Sar 2007
  [Fic]—dc22

                                                      2006039426

Design by Craig Oesterling
Cover photo: Stockphoto © Duncan Walker
Composition by Sherri Hartzler
© 2007 by BJU Press
Greenville, SC 29614
Printed in the United States of America
ISBN 978-1-59166-737-7

15 14 13 12 11 10 9 8 7 6 5 4 3 2 1

To Phoebe,

My youngest daughter, lover of horses and dogs.
When you are determined, there is no stopping you.
I know God will use this trait for good in your life.
You are much loved!

Mom

TABLE OF CONTENTS

I

Sarah Piper held her breath as Uncle Joe backed the horse trailer straight up to the open barn door, stopping in perfect position for unloading. Now if only Icicle and Clover could settle in quickly to their new life. Changes always unsettled horses, but she knew that if they adjusted well, things would go a lot smoother for her. New home, new guardian, maybe a new school—*Oh, please, Lord, I hope not*—and possibly new friends—*At least one, please. Please?*

She stepped forward and unlatched the back gate of the trailer, lowering it carefully to the ground to form a ramp for the two horses inside.

Icicle, Sarah's gray gelding, snorted and pawed impatiently inside the trailer.

"Hold on, boy, I'm going to get you out." She touched his hindquarters as she stepped up on the ramp and turned sideways to squeeze in beside him.

The door of the pickup closed and her uncle called, "All right in there?"

"We're fine," Sarah replied, but her hands shook as she hooked a blue nylon lead line to a ring in Icicle's halter. She didn't want to do anything to upset Uncle Joe. Living with him was going to be a big change for both of them, and until she got to know him better, she'd just as soon not make any mistakes.

"Dear Lord," she whispered, "Don't let Uncle Joe be sorry he brought us here. Help me to show him we won't cause him any trouble."

She unsnapped the chain that had secured the gelding's head during the seven-hour drive from northern California to the wilds of eastern Oregon. With one hand on the horse's velvety nose, she pulled on the halter.

"Back, boy, back."

Slowly, Icicle walked backward, snuffling and feeling for his footing. His hooves thudded on the boards. When they reached solid ground at the bottom of the ramp, Uncle Joe reached out and patted the gelding's shoulder.

"Nice-looking horse."

"Thanks," said Sarah, relief washing over her. "Where do I put him?"

"Second stall on the right." Uncle Joe mounted the ramp for the second horse, and Sarah turned Icicle to face the doorway to his new home.

From inside a fenced corral next to the barn, another horse neighed, and Icicle answered shrilly, tossing his head and looking toward the fence. Sarah held his halter firmly as the gelding began to prance.

"Take it easy, boy. You'll get the formal introductions later."

Half a dozen horses crowded against the rail fence, pawing and whinnying. Icicle and Clover would have plenty of company here.

What about me? Are there even any kids living out here? Will I find anyone to ride with?

She gulped and stroked Icicle's glossy gray neck, determined not to think about that now. "If we can't keep on competing, we'll just have to adjust, right, fella? At least we'll have plenty of territory to explore on our trail rides."

Uncle Joe's small, plain house was fifty yards away. The white paint was beginning to peel from the board siding. The barn looked newer, and the fences extended a long way. The natural rails were weathered to a soft gray. Across the road she saw only a hay field and distant mountains. It was so different from home, where she could see six or eight other houses from her front porch.

Sarah led her horse into the dim interior of the barn. The smells of timothy hay, oats, manure, and leather welcomed her. The tears that rushed to her eyes disconcerted her. This smelled like the stable at home, but she was pretty sure she'd never see or smell that little two-stall stable again. Her mother's death in a car accident last week had stunned Sarah and catapulted her into a whirl of changes.

She stopped Icicle for a moment and stood still, blinking. Between her tears and the dimness compared to the brilliant sun outside, it took her a moment to focus and locate the stall Uncle Joe had indicated was reserved for her horse.

Four box stalls lined each side of the wide dirt alley. On the left near the front door was a stall-sized niche serving as a tack room, with a feed room opposite it. A large loft overhead held baled hay, Sarah knew, and more was stacked in a lean-to on the right side of the barn.

The Dutch door to the second stall was open, and she led Icicle inside and turned him around, swinging the bottom half of the door closed behind them before releasing the horse. Sarah wiped her tears away with her sleeve.

Icicle immediately stretched to sniff the bedding on the floor, then raised his head and whinnied, pricking his ears forward as one of the horses in the corral responded, followed by a nicker from Clover, his old stablemate.

Uncle Joe led Clover into the barn and took her mare past them, to a stall on the opposite side of the aisle. Sarah left Icicle's stall, latching the door, and went to see how Clover was reacting to the new environment.

The solid, eleven-year-old bay mare had been Sarah's mother's mount. Clover and seven-year-old Icicle had gone many miles together.

Up until a week ago, Sarah and her mother trained almost every day for the long cross-country rides they competed in.

"Thanks for letting me bring Clover," she said, as Uncle Joe came out into the aisle, leaving the mare to explore her new surroundings.

"Extra work," he admitted with a shrug. "But, then, you said you'd handle it."

"I will. I promise."

He nodded. "Let's get these critters some water."

Sarah had visited her uncle's home in eastern Oregon a couple of times before and helped out in small ways in the barn when she was a guest. She knew where the faucet was, and when he handed her a black rubber bucket, she went to fill it for Icicle. When both horses had water, Uncle Joe brought two hay nets, and they filled them and hung them in the stalls.

"Tomorrow we'll let them out with the others," he said, and Sarah nodded. The simple routine of taking care of her horses had made her forget for a few minutes why they were there with Uncle Joe, but now it was time to go up to the house, and Sarah was jolted once more by the changes splintering her life.

Her uncle parked and unhitched the horse trailer, then walked toward the house without another word, and Sarah scurried after him.

She wished Uncle Joe would talk more. Sarah was used to discussing her day with her mother and making plans for the next day, while they prepared and ate supper together. Uncle Joe put two frozen dinners in the microwave oven without speaking and laid two knives, forks, and mugs on the table. Sarah automatically arranged them in place settings.

"You got napkins?" she asked tentatively.

He glanced toward her, then opened a cupboard and tossed her a roll of paper towels. Sarah tore off two, folded them in quarters and placed them next to the forks, while Uncle Joe watched with what she could only interpret as amusement.

"You a messy eater?"

She smiled. "Not generally."

Uncle Joe nodded. Sarah wondered if he thought she was up-pity for wanting napkins.

"I should have stopped at the store for some milk," he said.

"That's all right." Sarah filled her mug with water at the sink.

When the dinners were hot, Uncle Joe eased them from the microwave and plopped them on the table. "Beef or chicken?"

Sarah shrugged. "Either." Somehow it didn't seem right to say more since her uncle said so little.

He grunted and put the chicken down at Sarah's place. When they sat down, she watched him expectantly. She knew Uncle Joe believed in God. He had gone to church with them when he visited in California, and Sarah's mother had told her Uncle Joe was bap-tized when he was ten, with his older brother Dan, who was Sarah's father.

Uncle Joe eyed her, then looked away with a little shrug. "Don't usually pray out loud."

"I can pray," Sarah offered.

He nodded and closed his eyes.

Sarah bowed her head. "Lord, thank You for bringing us back here safe, and please bless this food, and help us know how to get along."

When she opened her eyes, Uncle Joe was watching her. It struck her anew that he looked like her father. Memories of Dad were hazy in her mind, but Uncle Joe seemed to clarify them just by being there.

When she thought back the eight years since her father's death, she remembered his dark hair and eyes the color of bitter choco-late. At thirty-three, Uncle Joe was a bit older than her father had been when he died, but not by much. And Uncle Joe was alive, but Dad was not, and that made looking at Uncle Joe much harder than looking at old pictures of Dad.

"You okay?" he asked, and she knew she'd been staring at him.

"Yes, sir." She forced the words past the lump in her throat and blinked at the tears that welled once more in her eyes.

He grimaced. "Don't call me sir."

"Okay."

He picked up his fork. "I don't know if this life will suit you. Maybe I was crazy to bring a fourteen-year-old girl out here in the middle of nowhere." He attacked the roast beef on his plastic plate.

"It's a wonderful place. I thank you for taking me in, Uncle Joe."

He shrugged. "I still think it's the best thing, but I don't know how it's gonna turn out. We need to talk about school."

Sarah's heart plummeted. It was early August, and in four weeks the public schools would open. Her mother had taught her at home, but Uncle Joe had already made it clear that he didn't feel competent to teach a girl going into ninth grade.

"I brought my books. I'm pretty self-sufficient now, really." Sarah had helped her mother choose the new textbooks in June, and they had ordered them from the publisher. English grammar, literature, algebra, earth science, government, and Spanish. There were cassette tapes to go with the Spanish book, and a solution key for the algebra.

"We'll talk about it," he said.

When they had eaten, Uncle Joe threw the plastic dishes in the trash and rinsed the silverware at the sink. He left his coffee mug, unwashed, on the drain board.

Sarah watched him carefully, eager to learn her uncle's routines so she wouldn't disrupt them and upset him. If she were too much trouble, Uncle Joe might not want to keep her, and there were only so many other options.

Grandma and Grandpa Anderson lived in a retirement home, and her Piper grandparents were dead. Uncle Joe's sister, Aunt Natalie, lived in downtown Portland. She had offered doubtfully

6

to "help with the girl," but Sarah knew that if she went to live with Aunt Natalie there would be no barn, and Icicle and Clover would not go with her.

Her mother had a sister too. Aunt Marjorie and her husband had flown in all the way from Pennsylvania last week for the funeral. Aunt Marjorie had been very upset by her sister's death and had hugged Sarah and offered sympathy, but no real comfort. Sarah had felt skittish around her, avoiding her tearful gaze and wondering if she would have to go East to live.

She remembered Uncle Joe taking her aside the morning of the funeral.

"Sarah, seems to me the best thing is for you to come back to Elk Creek with me, and bring that nag along. You fly off to Pennsylvania, and you've got no horse."

Sarah had gulped for air as she processed the offer he was making. The question of what would become of Icicle and Clover had been heavy on her mind.

"Yes, sir." She tried to keep her voice from shaking. A cowboy like Uncle Joe wouldn't want a crying female around all the time.

"Same with my sister, Natalie," Uncle Joe said. "No place to keep a horse there."

"No, sir."

"A girl ought not to lose her mother and her horse at the same time."

"No, sir."

"Don't call me sir."

"No, s—Uncle Joe."

"All right then."

She didn't know what he said to Aunt Natalie and Aunt Marjorie, but they both seemed relieved, and it was settled. By late afternoon the aunts had hugged her and gone away.

Uncle Joe stayed in California with her three more days after her mother's funeral. They sorted and packed everything in the house and talked to a lawyer. Uncle Joe dealt with the landlord of the suburban house her mother had rented and took Sarah to the bank to close her mother's accounts. He suggested tentatively that they ought to place an ad right away to sell Clover, and Sarah had balked.

"I'd like to keep Mom's horse, Uncle Joe."

"Well, I've only got so much space."

"I know, but—" Sarah didn't know how to say what she felt. Icicle and Clover were best friends. To separate them after five years together would be cruel, Sarah thought. And Clover was in top condition for long distance rides.

In the days since her mother's death, Sarah hadn't been able to think ahead to whether or not she would still be competing. It seemed too frivolous somehow to think about distance rides in a time of tragedy.

Her entire world had exploded when she'd learned that her mother was dead, and her heart was ragged from crying and trying to understand what had happened. But she knew that eventually she would want to ride again and would want to go on with the sport she and her parents had enjoyed so much.

Without an adult sponsor and a horse for that sponsor to ride, Sarah wouldn't be allowed to compete again. With Clover, her goal was still viable, even though she didn't feel like training right now. She knew that, in time, riding would be her consolation, and she didn't want to slam the door on the competition she loved.

2

After supper Uncle Joe went to take the horses in from the corral. Sarah learned that he was training four of them for customers. After bedding them down in their stalls, he went back out for his own two mounts. Sarah grabbed the halter on the wiry pinto, Ranger, and Uncle Joe took the larger black quarter horse, Zorro.

A man drove up in a dust-covered gray pickup as they walked the horses toward the barn.

"Hey, Joe, I figured you'd be back, but I thought I'd check," the driver called as he climbed out of the truck. He was taller than Uncle Joe, all long arms and legs, and his stained felt hat was the same color as his truck.

Uncle Joe paused for a moment, holding Zorro's lead line. "We're all set. Thanks for feeding these nags while I was gone."

"No problem." The man followed them into the barn. "Say, you've got some new horseflesh."

"Yup. Belongs to my niece, Sarah." Uncle Joe jerked his head toward her.

"Howdy." The man touched the brim of his hat.

"Hi." Sarah darted him a glance and turned Ranger into the only available stall.

"Good-looking horse." The tall cowboy leaned on the half door of Icicle's stall, seeming very much at home in Uncle Joe's barn.

"Thank you, sir." Pride swelled inside Sarah as she peeked in at the glossy gray horse. His coal black mane and tail reflected glints of light.

Uncle Joe laughed. "Don't call him sir. Junior won't know who you're talking to."

"I'm Junior Tate," the man said. "That your horse?"

"Yes."

"Do you run cattle with him?"

"No, sir."

"It's Junior."

Sarah nodded, though the name seemed odd. The man's weathered face and the graying hair peaking from beneath his cowboy hat told her he was probably a generation older than Uncle Joe.

"I mostly ride trail with him," she said. "My mom and I did distance riding."

"What, those hundred-mile cavalry ride things?"

Sarah smiled. "Well, I never did do a hundred-miler, but I was planning to. We mostly did fifties and twenty-fives. We did one seventy-five-miler last summer."

"Yeah?" Junior pushed his hat back and looked Sarah up and down. "You win anything?"

"Not much. A couple of belt buckles and a halter. But my mom won the trophy for best-conditioned horse at the Dry Branch Ride in June."

"That so?"

"Yes, that's her horse." Sarah nodded toward Clover's stall.

Junior ambled across the aisle, dodging Uncle Joe, who was bringing in hay for his horses.

"Well, now, that little mare ain't so pretty."

"No, sir, but she's tough," Sarah said, springing to Clover's defense. "She can go fifty miles without even breathing hard."

"How old is she?"

"Eleven. My mom had her a long time. She went on a lot of rides with Clover."

Junior nodded. "That one would make a good cow pony. So, you going to keep on doing those rides now?"

Sarah looked down at the floor and kicked at a small mound of hay Uncle Joe had dropped. "I don't know. We haven't talked about it yet."

"You staying with Joe for a while?" Junior asked, his voice lower.

"Yes, sir. I mean, Junior."

Junior eyed her the way he had the horses. "Well, you probably oughta know, Joe ain't much for contests. Never could get him to do anything like that. No horse shows or rodeos or anything. He just trains other folks' horses to do that. He does what he does, and he does good."

Sarah nodded. She thought she understood, although Junior's way of putting things was a bit unorthodox. Uncle Joe was a good trainer, and he didn't have to show off for people to know that.

"But he might let you go to rides," Junior said. "You just never know."

"Well, if he won't go with me, I can't." Sarah cleared her throat, determined not to let a whine creep into her voice. "You have to have an adult with you."

"That so?"

"Yes, sir. Kids under sixteen have to stay with their sponsor on the ride, and you have to finish within a minute of the sponsor."

Junior whistled. "So your momma stuck with you, even when she could have won, I'll bet."

"Maybe," Sarah conceded. "She didn't really care so much about winning. Just doing it was fun, you know?" She looked up into Junior's pale blue eyes. The cowboy was lanky and loose-jointed. Sarah guessed he spent a lot of time in the saddle.

"Do you live around here?" she asked.

"Yup, next place east of here. I run some beef on my ranch. Joe and I get along. He asked me to feed for him while he went to bury his sister. I reckon you're what's left of the family."

"That's right. My father died when I was six."

"Joe's brother?"

"Yes—" she finally succeeded in swallowing the *sir*. It surprised her that she could talk about it with him, and she hadn't broken down in tears yet.

"You an only child?"

"Yes, I am."

"Well, Joe's not much for talking either." Junior glanced down the aisle toward his friend, who was disappearing into a stall where a client's Appaloosa mare crunched her evening meal. "If you get lonesome and need to talk to someone who'll talk back, you just let me know, you hear?"

"Sure. Do you have any kids, Mr. Tate?"

"Nope, not married. And it's Junior. But I'm not bad for someone to talk to. And the neighbor on the other side of me, Rose Zucker, she's a good one for talking too. Or should I say listening?"

Hope sprang up in Sarah's heart. "Does Mrs. Zucker have kids?"

"Well, no, not the kind you're thinking of."

Sarah nodded, trying not to show her disappointment. Elk Creek sat in a desolate area, with ranches spread out across the dry land. It took a good many acres to support an animal in the sagebrush and juniper country, let alone earn enough to support a family. There might not be any other young people within miles.

Uncle Joe came out of the Appaloosa's stall and walked toward them.

"If you two lunkheads are done yapping, you can help me unload Sarah's gear."

Junior and Sarah followed him out to the pickup. They each grabbed a saddle, and Uncle Joe brought the bridles and the bucket of brushes and tools.

"Better drive up to the house with the rest," he muttered.

They all piled in, and he drove to the front steps, then got out, swung the tailgate down, and hefted his own duffel bag and Sarah's two suitcases to the ground. Sarah picked up her two bags and carried them inside to the empty spare room he had shown her earlier.

When she went back into the kitchen, Junior was bringing in boxes. She hadn't kept much, but Uncle Joe had encouraged her to save her mother's files, and to bring along the family photo albums and any other small items she wanted to keep.

Her mother's best friend, Becky Moseley, had agreed to dispose of Laura's clothing for them, but she had advised Sarah to keep her mother's wedding and engagement rings and a few pieces of her jewelry and china. Her mother's endurance riding trophies and ribbons had also come with Sarah.

"You'll have children yourself someday, Sarah, and you'll be proud to give them something that was your mother's," Becky had explained.

Uncle Joe hadn't protested and had found boxes for her to pack things in. Now the two men unloaded them and took them to Sarah's new room.

A window looked out over the driveway from the small room toward the barn and the corral. Sarah was glad. She could look out and see if Uncle Joe's truck was in the yard and watch the horses when they were out to graze. The walls were painted a pale gray, almost the color of Icicle's glossy coat, and there was no curtain at the window, just a white roller shade.

When the boxes were unloaded, Uncle Joe pulled the pieces of Sarah's bed from the truck. He had warned her that he had no extra bed at home, and they had taken Sarah's single bed apart and packed it first in the pickup. They'd brought her dresser too, and a small bookcase her father had built the first year her parents were married. The rest of the furniture had gone in the truck of a used furniture dealer, and Uncle Joe had pocketed the check, promising to open a bank account for Sarah when they were settled in Elk Creek.

Somewhere in the boxes were the sheets that fit Sarah's bed. While Junior and Uncle Joe put the bed together, she rummaged for them. At last she found the blue set with unicorns galloping up and down it. They seemed childish all of a sudden, and she dug deeper, coming up with a set of brown and blue plaid sheets. She left the unicorn ones in the box. After Uncle Joe and Junior plopped the mattress onto the frame, she began making the bed.

"Need some help?" Junior asked.

"No, sir, I can do it."

"Want coffee?" Uncle Joe slid the last drawer into the dresser, and Sarah knew he was asking Junior.

"Well, natch," said Junior. "Hey, I've got doughnuts in my truck."

"Where'd you get doughnuts?" Uncle Joe asked.

"Went to town this afternoon."

The two men went out of the room, and it seemed a little bigger then. Sarah made the bed up and stood looking at the boxes. She would unpack her books and the rest of her clothes tomorrow, she decided. She dragged the other boxes to the closet and shoved them in on the floor, then closed the door.

Slowly she walked down the short hallway, past the bathroom and Uncle Joe's room, to the large kitchen-living room.

Junior was perched backward on a kitchen chair, telling a story that involved a pony and several Angus steers, waving a doughnut around as he talked, punctuating his sentences with sips of coffee. A box of a dozen doughnuts sat open on the table between them, and Uncle Joe slouched in his chair, smiling faintly and working away at his own coffee and a jelly doughnut.

"Hey, Sarah, better get yourself a doughnut before Joe eats them all," Junior called.

She smiled and went to the cupboard for a plate, then thought better of it and got a paper towel instead. She was mentally building a list of things Uncle Joe wasn't *much for*, as Junior would say, and washing dishes was near the top. The doughnuts were good, but a little dry from sitting in Junior's truck for a couple of hours. She wished she had a glass of milk, but settled for water from the tap.

"Well, guess I'd better mosey on," Junior said when they were down to two doughnuts. Sarah was sure by now he was talking that way to be funny. Things he'd said during the conversation told her he wasn't stupid, but he seemed to want her to think he was an ignorant cowpoke.

"Keep the rest of those for your breakfast." He turned to Sarah. "Don't let Joe eat yours now, will ya?"

"No, sir."

"All right." Junior stood up, clapping his beat-up hat onto his head. "Well, kid, I'm sorry about your mother."

Sarah looked at the bare maple table. "Thank you."

"I'll see you Sunday, if not before."

Uncle Joe nodded, and Junior looked woefully at both of them.

"Goodbye." Sarah stood up, uncertain as to ranching etiquette. Uncle Joe remained slumped in his chair.

"What's Sunday?" she asked, when the door had banged behind Junior.

"Church," said Uncle Joe.

"Mr. Tate goes to your church?"

"Yes." Uncle Joe sipped his coffee.

Sarah smiled. "At least there'll be someone else I know at church then."

"Miss Rose will be there too."

"The neighbor beyond Mr. Tate?"

"Uh-huh. She and Junior have been ranching side by side for nigh on thirty years now, and Junior does a lot of chores for her."

"So they're old friends."

"Yes, and good friends for anyone to have. If you ever get in a fix, and I can't help you, go to them, you hear?"

Sarah nodded, wondering what situation that might be. She supposed that if Uncle Joe were injured, or if he were away on business and she needed help, a neighbor might be very handy. "What's Miss Rose like?"

"You'll see her Sunday." He got up and carried his mug and Junior's to the sink and rinsed Junior's.

Sarah hadn't heard Uncle Joe talk so much since the day they'd met with the lawyer, the banker, and the landlord. The long drive to Elk Creek had been mostly silent, except for the pickup's engine as it toiled over the Cascade Mountains.

"What does he do for her?" she asked.

"Puts up hay for her critters and hauls water when her well goes dry."

"Does she pay him?"

"She pays him back with pies and tolerance."

That seemed like an odd friendship to Sarah.

Uncle Joe went out, and Sarah pulled in a deep breath. She was sure he wasn't going farther than the barn, but she couldn't help shivering. What if he got in his truck and drove off without telling her where he was going?

She dashed to the window and stared out into the twilight. She saw her uncle stand in the barn doorway for a moment, then turn and slide the big door shut. He headed back toward the house, and she jumped away from the window.

Taking a shaky breath, she scolded herself inwardly. She was acting like a baby. Uncle Joe wasn't going to leave her alone here.

He simply wasn't used to having another person around and the idea of telling anyone what he was going to do next. She didn't want to be a bother to him. She would just have to watch him and get used to his ways, that was all. Somehow she had to fit into his life here on the ranch without disrupting his routine. Because she did want to stay.

3

Early in the morning Sarah heard her uncle moving quietly about the house. She groped for her wristwatch. Five thirty. Too early. She rolled over and went back to sleep. An hour later she woke again and rolled out of bed. When she looked out the window, she saw that the barn door was open, and the horses, including Icicle and Clover, were in the pasture.

She rushed to pull on her jeans, boots, and a T-shirt. She had promised Uncle Joe she would care for her own mounts, and she didn't want him to think she was slacking off already. In the bathroom she raked her brush through her short, sandy hair. She ran down the hallway and catapulted out the door. A few seconds later she skidded to a stop in the barn doorway, gasping for breath.

"Morning." Uncle Joe was pushing a wheelbarrow of manure and soiled bedding toward the back door of the barn.

"Sorry I slept late."

"It's not late." He disappeared out the back door, and Sarah went to a tool rack and selected a shovel. When Uncle Joe came back with the wheelbarrow, she was at work in Icicle's stall.

"You can use this." He parked the wheelbarrow within easy reach for her.

"Thanks."

"I fed your nags."

"Thanks. You didn't have to."

"Well, it was easier to feed them all at once. I generally feed early and put them out, except the ones I'm going to work with."

Sarah glanced down the row of stalls and saw a gray Arabian and a pinto peering over their stall doors, their ears pricked with curiosity. The pinto chewed a mouthful of hay and stared at her. The Arabian nickered and stretched its neck, sniffing the air.

"She's pretty," Sarah said.

"Mm, that mare's Dulcet. She belongs to a rich lady in Salem. They had me go over and get her and bring her out here for a month of training."

"What are you training her to do?"

"Be a trail horse."

"That's pretty funny." Sarah leaned on the handle of her shovel. "Why doesn't the owner just ride her on trails?"

"No, she wants her to win trail classes in horse shows," Uncle Joe explained. "Big difference."

"Oh."

"She was doing fine in Western Pleasure classes, but there was no way she'd go over a wooden bridge."

Sarah understood about horses and bridges. It was something she and her mother had worked hard on with Clover and Icicle, until both horses trotted confidently over them with no hesitation.

"You finish your cleanup and come out to the ring, and I'll show you how much progress Dulcet's made."

Sarah went back to work, and a moment later saw Uncle Joe pass her carrying a black saddle and a western bridle with a fat snaffle bit. By the time she had finished cleaning Icicle's stall and put down more wood shavings for bedding, he had taken the mare outside. Sarah hurried to take care of Clover's stall. Clover wasn't as messy as Icicle, and she was soon finished.

Outside she dumped the wheelbarrow's contents on the manure · pile and went eagerly to the fence that bordered the training ring on the far side of the barn and hay shed.

In the middle of the ring were several plastic barrels, some orange cones, a low wooden bridge, and a series of cavaletti, low hurdles that horses could step over. The bridge didn't span anything, just grass. Sarah knew Uncle Joe used it to accustom horses to the sound of their hooves echoing on the boards. Many horses were frightened by the hollow sound and refused to take bridges.

The dappled gray mare wore the eye-catching black western tack, and Uncle Joe was trotting her around the edge of the ring. When Sarah climbed up on the weathered board fence, he waved and took Dulcet to the middle of the ring, lining her body up straight toward the bridge. She walked at an even, measured pace, not hesitating the slightest bit. When she stepped up onto the boards and her hooves struck with a loud, hollow thudding, she went on without flinching, over the slight arch and down the other side to the grass again. Uncle Joe urged her into an easy lope and brought her around to where Sarah sat on the fence.

"Pretty good," Sarah said with approval, reaching out to scratch the mare's forehead. "How long have you been working with her?"

"Her time's almost up. I was afraid she'd backslide while I was away." He had been in northern California and on the road for nearly a week, Sarah knew. Uncle Joe had left his ranch as soon as Becky Moseley called him and told him about Mom's fatal car accident, showing up on the Moseleys' doorstep at five the next morning. That had meant a lot to Sarah, to know someone in her family cared enough to drive all night to come to her.

He slapped the mare on the neck. "I'm pretty happy with her. We'll take her back next Monday."

"I get to go?" Sarah asked in surprise.

"Unless you want to stay here."

"No, I'd like to go with you."

"It's a long haul, but we'll leave early, after we feed, and be back before dark. Should be all right."

Sarah nodded, stroking Dulcet's velvety nose. "Uncle Joe, I'd like to take Icicle out for a while this morning. Is that okay? I need to keep him and Clover in shape. Clover hasn't been ridden all week."

Uncle Joe nodded. "That pinto in the barn needs some work. I can go along if you like, show you some trails."

"Thanks."

"Let's get some breakfast." Uncle Joe rode the Arabian over to the gate. Sarah was going to open it for him, but realized this was also part of Dulcet's training. Uncle Joe moved her parallel to the gate and leaned down to unlatch it, then rode through, keeping his hand on the top of the swinging gate. Cueing the horse with his legs, he kept her close to the gate, moving her sideways as he shut it, and hooked the latch.

Sarah held her breath. The mare was perfect in her routine. Uncle Joe dismounted and led Dulcet toward the barn, where he unsaddled her. Removing the bridle, he snapped her into cross ties, one line coming out from the wall on each side of the aisle, to keep her immobile while he worked on her. He brushed her down quickly and ran his hands down her legs, lifting each foot for a moment.

"Bet she cleans up at the horse shows," Sarah said.

"Hope so. Most owners wait 'til the season's over to send them for training. I think Mrs. Randolph was getting frustrated with her. I'm hoping Dulcet's calmed down enough to win now. But horses pick up the rider's attitude. Mrs. Randolph needs to be calm too."

Sarah nodded, knowing the truth of that.

"The proof will be in the moment she enters the show ring." He unhooked Dulcet and led her out to the pasture, releasing her to graze with the other horses.

After breakfast Sarah stood inside the gate and whistled, and Icicle came to her and nuzzled her plaid shirt. Clover came too and stood next to the gelding, swishing her tail.

"You want me to ride that mare?" Uncle Joe asked as he opened the gate.

"That's okay. I can take her out later."

"Well, I need to work the pinto, but I can always do that when we get back, if these two are best buddies."

"They are, but I think she'll be all right. She doesn't jump fences or anything." Sarah had often taken Icicle out to ride alone at home while her mother was working at the computer on her magazine articles, and Clover had stayed behind without making too big a fuss.

Uncle Joe nodded. "She's a hotshot endurance horse, isn't that right? Your mother told me on the phone once how good the mare is."

"Yes, sir. She's not purebred, and I guess she doesn't look all that special, but she's got heart."

Uncle Joe stroked Clover's muzzle. "Well, my sister-in-law set a lot of store by her, I know that."

That seemed to be high praise, and Sarah's spirits rose a little. She'd never been sure how Uncle Joe felt about her and her mother. They'd lived so far from him, they'd only seen him a few times in the eight years since her father's death.

They turned back to the barn, and while Sarah tacked Icicle up, Uncle Joe led out Rocky and snapped the cross ties to his halter.

"Is that a show horse too?" Sarah asked skeptically. The black and white pinto's conformation was not what a judge would look for. The stocky gelding was slightly potbellied, and he had a decidedly Roman nose.

"No, no, this is just a plain old hoss." He tossed a striped woven blanket over Rocky's back. "His owner just wants me to put a few manners into him, so he'll be safe when his daughter rides him. I told him he'd better get the girl some training too, so he brings her around twice a week for her lesson. She'll be coming this afternoon. That's why I wanted to work him this morning. I don't want him to be too fresh when the little girl gets on him, and he hasn't been ridden all the time I was gone."

"How old is the girl?" Sarah asked.

"Eight."

Sarah was disappointed. She had hoped to meet someone her own age, and already she missed her best friend, Eric, the Moseleys' son. When Becky Moseley started riding with Mom after Sarah's father died, Sarah and Eric saw a lot of each other. They were the same age, and both had been taught at home by their mothers. After Mom had talked Becky into entering a twenty-five-mile ride with her, the two families were inseparable, and Sarah began calling Eric's mother "Aunt Becky."

The summer Sarah and Eric had turned nine, the Moseleys bought two horses, and then the two youngsters trained with their mothers for endurance riding. They had ridden trails together almost daily. Sarah rode her father's old horse at first. Later she got Icicle, and he and Eric's gelding, Hannibal, were practically blood brothers, they spent so much time together.

Leaving the Moseleys behind in California had been very difficult for Sarah. Aunt Becky was a lot like her mother, and Mr. Moseley had supported them all in their chosen sport, although he didn't ride himself.

Eric had made Sarah promise to write when she left with Uncle Joe and to e-mail him if her uncle had a computer, but Sarah hadn't seen one yet in the house. In fact she hadn't seen much in the way of electronics.

"Have you got a TV, Uncle Joe?"

"Nope." Uncle Joe slipped a curb bit into the pinto's mouth, and Sarah cinched Icicle's saddle girth.

"How about a computer?" she asked without much hope as she took the lead line off Icicle's bridle and led him out of the stall.

"Nope."

Sarah sighed. It figured. She led Icicle outside and swung up into the saddle. Uncle Joe led Rocky out and mounted, then looked at her keenly.

"I'm not much on gadgets," he said.

Sarah nodded. "It's okay."

"You like TV?"

She shrugged. "I don't need it."

"What about the computer? Do you need that for school?"

"Not really." Sarah gulped. It was the first thing Uncle Joe had said that indicated he was thinking about the possibility of Sarah continuing her education at home. "I was just thinking I could e-mail Eric if you had a computer."

"That the Moseley boy? Where you stayed last week?"

Sarah nodded.

She had been at the Moseleys' house when the call came about Mom's accident. Aunt Becky and Eric had driven her to the hospital and had stayed with her when she heard the terrible news that her mother was dead. They had insisted she go back home with them until relatives arrived. Aunt Becky had stopped at the Pipers' house so Sarah could get a few clothes and Mom's address book, then she had called Grandpa Anderson and Uncle Joe while Sarah sat by shivering and trying not to cry.

Aunt Becky, Eric, and Eric's dad, Peter Moseley, had sat up late with Sarah that night and cried with her. Eric, suddenly shy, had tried to express his empathy.

"I can't imagine how much you're hurting," he'd whispered, tears streaming down his cheeks.

At five the next morning, Uncle Joe had arrived at the Moseleys' house. Sarah ran down the steps in her pajamas and flung herself into his arms, feeling helpless and childish, but better somehow, seeing Uncle Joe so solid and ordinary in his faded jeans and black Stetson.

"Hope it's not too early, ma'am," he'd said apologetically to Aunt Becky, who stood in the doorway in her housecoat.

"No, of course not," Aunt Becky said, although they had been up late and dark circles of fatigue edged her eyes. "Would you like some coffee, Mr. Piper? My husband has to work today, and I was just about to make breakfast."

Now that she was at Uncle Joe's ranch to stay, Sarah was feeling the double loss of her mother and her friends. Eric and his parents had been through that first awful shock with her and had shown her their love and compassion. They had insisted that Sarah stay in the comfort and familiarity of their home until Uncle Joe was ready to take her back to the ranch, even though Uncle Joe and the other relatives who came slept at a motel a few miles away.

Sarah put thoughts of Eric and his family aside as they rode out of the barnyard and concentrated on her new surroundings. The land was much more open here than what she was used to, and browner. She rode beside Uncle Joe for a couple of miles along hillsides that grew increasingly steep. The horses jogged steadily through sagebrush and scattered swatches of stunted dry grass, not following a trail.

Icicle kept turning his head to see his new companion. He was full of bounce, and Sarah had to work hard to keep him in hand. When Rocky came close beside them, Icicle flattened his ears and reached out to snap his teeth in the pinto's face.

"Hey, none of that." Sarah slapped Icicle affectionately on the side of his neck opposite where the black mane fell. "He's not vicious," she said to Uncle Joe.

"Nope."

Sarah smiled. Conversing with her uncle was a real challenge. Her father hadn't been that way, at least she didn't remember him as taciturn, but then, Sarah had been only six when her father died. Funny how brothers could be so alike, yet so different. She'd heard Uncle Joe talk to the horses, but not nonstop the way Eric did with his Hannibal. Uncle Joe mostly talked to them through his hands,

Sarah thought, but when a word was needed, he gave it. That and no more.

On the horizon she made out a stand of trees, and as they drew closer she saw that it was a large patch of jack pine. They rode down a hillside and hit a trail, plunging into the shade. Down and down the path went between the pines, not steeply, but a steady descent, and soon over the sounds of creaking leather and snuffling horses she could hear running water.

Uncle Joe rode ahead of her on the path, and Sarah kept Icicle back, so the gelding wouldn't bump Rocky's tail. At the bottom of the slope they came upon the stream she had heard. The water ran fast over its rocky bed, churning into white foam, and the trail ran toward a log bridge that spanned the stream.

Uncle Joe pushed Rocky toward the bridge. The pinto checked, as if he would stop, but Uncle Joe urged him on, squeezing the horse's sides with his legs. Rocky flicked his ears and stepped onto the bridge. He jumped a little at the reverberation and skittered quickly to the other side.

Sarah held Icicle back until she was sure the pinto would cross without balking, then she walked him straight toward the bridge.

The gray gelding tossed his head and snorted, but didn't pause. Sarah felt a rush of pride as they crossed the bridge at the same steady pace they had used to approach it. Uncle Joe had stopped and turned his horse around so he could watch them cross. As Sarah and Icicle came up to him, he nodded and turned Rocky to continue.

They rode out of the trees soon, and Uncle Joe took them in a large loop. They crossed the stream again lower down, where it was lazier and the horses could wade across. An hour later, when they jogged back into the barnyard, he looked at Sarah.

"You can ride down there anytime. It's safe. Part of it's Junior's land, and the part with the woods is BLM land."

Sarah nodded. She knew local ranchers relied heavily on acreage owned by the Bureau of Land Management for grazing.

"Is your mother's horse safe on bridges too?"

"Yes, sir."

Uncle Joe nodded and dismounted, leading Rocky in and hooking him in the cross ties. Sarah took Icicle to his stall and pulled the saddle off, then removed the bridle and brushed him. She checked the horse's feet and brought him a bucket of tepid water. While she carried out the routine tasks, Sarah felt comforted somehow. She wouldn't be lonely here with Icicle and Clover and Uncle Joe, even if all of them were quiet.

Uncle Joe loved horses the same way Sarah's father had, or perhaps even more. The strangeness was wearing off, and she was glad Uncle Joe looked like his older brother, or like Sarah seemed to remember him looking. Same dark hair and deep brown eyes. It wasn't the same as having Dad back, but it felt right.

"Are you taking the mare out after lunch?" he asked.

"If that's okay with you."

"Sure. Just be careful. I'll show you some more trails tomorrow afternoon."

"Okay, thanks."

The next day would be Sunday, and Sarah realized she'd have more adjustments to make. A new church, a new pastor, a new Sunday school class. She hoped there would be girls her age.

4

When Sarah took Clover out for exercise that afternoon, Uncle Joe was giving the eight-year-old girl her lesson on Rocky in the riding ring. Her parents leaned on the fence and watched, and Rocky seemed to be behaving.

Sarah took Clover over the same ground they had covered that morning. The mare was frisky, and Sarah let her lope along the hillsides toward Junior's land. When they came to the bridge, Clover stepped confidently onto it, clopping sedately to the other side, then picked up the pace with an extended trot. When they emerged from the woods, she broke into a lope again.

No one had ridden Clover since Laura Piper's last training ride. Sarah wondered if Clover missed Mom in some equine way. If she was going to keep the mare and Icicle both in top shape, she'd have to work hard. Staying fit for endurance rides required hours of trail riding day after day. Was it worth it? She might never have a chance to compete again.

She was at the farthest point from Uncle Joe's ranch, about to turn toward home on the backstretch of the loop, when she saw a chestnut quarter horse with a white blaze cantering toward her across a meadow. Sarah pulled Clover to a stop and watched the horse until the rider waved and she recognized Junior Tate.

"Hey, kid," Junior called.

He was inside a fenced range, and far behind him, near the crest of a knoll, Sarah could see a few Angus cattle grazing.

She walked Clover over, close to the fence. "Hello, Mr. Tate!"

"That's your momma's mare, right?"

"Yes, sir."

"It's Junior."

"Right."

"She looks better under saddle."

"Thanks. Uncle Joe said I could ride out here. I hope you don't mind."

"Not a bit. I've got some other trails you can ride too. You heading back to Joe's now?"

"Yes."

"Well, about half a mile along you'll see a fork to the right."

"I saw it this morning," Sarah said.

"Well, that fork goes to a spring. If you keep going past the spring, it'll come out on the state road after a while. You'd be about three miles from home when you hit the road. Turn left at the road if you do that."

"Thanks."

"There's mostly plenty of room to ride along at the side of the road, if you ever want to go that way. Not as good as the trails, but it's something different to look at."

"Great. I need to figure out some long rides I can train these horses on, twenty miles or so at a time."

"Hm. You'd probably ought to have someone along if you're going that far."

"Yes," Sarah said, a bit discouraged. Her mother hadn't let her ride so far alone either, but usually Mom or Eric or Aunt Becky had been eager to train too. It was going to be harder now, and Sarah had two horses to work. "Uncle Joe came with me this morning, but he's busy now giving a riding lesson."

Junior nodded. "He takes some of the horses he's training out on the trails. His two need exercise too. Likely he'll ride with you some."

"He said he will tomorrow," Sarah agreed.

"Well, call me if you need a partner one day next week. Or maybe Rose Zucker would go out with you. She borrows one of my ponies when she wants to ride."

"Thanks." Sarah was glad Junior seemed willing to help her out, but she realized she was hoping Uncle Joe would be the one spending time with her that fall. She wanted to get to know him better and to show him that she was a Piper too. She didn't look like the Pipers; her light hair and blue eyes guaranteed that she didn't look like Uncle Joe and her father. But that didn't matter so much, she decided. Family was a lot more than that. There was something else there between them, if only Uncle Joe would acknowledge it. They belonged together. Not only was she his niece, but Sarah took horses seriously, the way he did. Riding was more than a hobby for her. More and more she thought she wanted to make horses her career. Uncle Joe would understand that, the way her mother had.

Junior turned the chestnut away with a wave, and Sarah rode back to the trail. At the fork she decided to take Clover to explore the spring.

The new trail was shady and cool. Clover walked along lazily for half a mile, switching her tail at flies. Then she perked up, snuffling, and strained forward.

"You smell water, girl?" Sarah asked, stroking her neck. She let the mare jog, and in a few strides they were within sight of the spring. The water trickled off in a languid stream, and Sarah thought that eventually it must join the stream that ran under the bridge.

She dismounted and let Clover drink deeply.

"What do you say, girl?" she asked, checking the saddle girth. "Should we ride out to the road, or head back on the trail?"

She pulled Clover's head up and swung onto her back, deciding to stick with the trails. They went back to the fork and headed home, the way Uncle Joe had showed her that morning.

The family that owned Rocky had left by the time she got back, and Uncle Joe was turning the pinto out to pasture.

"How'd the lesson go?"

"Fine." He closed the gate. "How was your ride?"

"Great. And I saw Junior." Sarah swung down from the saddle. "Clover was a little eager, but she did fine."

For the rest of the afternoon she watched Uncle Joe work with the other clients' horses in the ring. The palomino was so polished, she wondered what Uncle Joe could possibly teach him. The Appaloosa mare, Penny, had a rough trot, and Uncle Joe lunged her, standing in the center of the ring and having the mare circle him at the end of a long line, working on her gaits. Sarah was impressed by the way he got the horses to obey his voice. After a while he saddled the mare and forced her to change leads at a canter. Penny didn't like it, but she obeyed Uncle Joe's firm touch.

As Sarah watched, her admiration for her uncle grew, and she longed to take instruction from him in riding and training horses. Icicle already had been trained to the saddle when her mother bought the horse for Sarah five years ago, but the gelding was only two years old then. Sarah had done all of Icicle's training for long-distance riding.

Horses were barred from endurance riding until they turned five, so during Icicle's early years of growth and maturing, Sarah had ridden the old chestnut her father had owned and competed on. But Icicle had claimed her heart from the first day she saw him. She'd started out giving the colt easy workouts as his muscles and bones grew. For the past two years she had trained him harder, and they rode in fifty- and seventy-five-mile rides with her mother, Aunt Becky, and Eric.

This year was to have been the big test for them all. They had done well in a fifty-miler in June and planned to compete in late August in their first one-hundred-mile ride. Mom hadn't entered such a strenuous event since Dad's death, and the others were keyed up with excitement for their first one hundred-miler. They were confident that they could complete the course. Sarah knew Icicle would excel. She dreamed of the four of them finishing in the top ten riders.

But that was before the accident.

Uncle Joe was finished working the handsome Appaloosa mare, and he brought her out into the barnyard and walked her up and down to cool her off. "This one's rough," he said. "I haven't had her long."

Sarah was a little surprised at how much her uncle was talking to her now. Maybe he'd just needed time to get used to having another person around.

"How long will it take to teach her everything?"

He laughed. "Can't ever teach 'em everything. Penny will be passable in another month, but she'll never be smooth, like my Zorro."

"Can you teach me to do that?"

Uncle Joe stopped walking and stared at her, one eyebrow raised, then walked on with a chuckle, leading Penny. "Teach you to change leads?"

Sarah laughed. "Yeah, right."

He turned and winked at her. "You just never know."

That night Sarah spent an hour unpacking her clothes and books. She pulled an array of shoes from a cardboard box and lined them up on the closet floor next to her riding boots. Would she ever wear sandals or ballet flats again?

She smoothed the wrinkles from the skirt of a linen dress with her hand, but they refused to disappear that easily. Did Uncle Joe have an iron? She doubted it. A man who wore only jeans and soft, frayed shirts wouldn't need an iron. At least he had a washing machine, though there didn't seem to be a drier. From the bathroom window she'd spotted a clothesline behind the house.

She set her unused ninth grade schoolbooks on the top shelf of the bookcase. If Uncle Joe made her go to school, maybe she could ship them back to the publisher for a refund. She hoped it wouldn't come to that. The idea of a long bus ride every morning and afternoon repelled her. She would miss out on hours of potential horseback riding time.

Tucked in with the textbooks was her mother's Bible. She took it from the box and ran her fingertips over the nubbly leather cover. In the lower right corner, embossed in gold, was the name Laura Piper. Sarah caressed the letters and took a deep breath.

I won't cry again. If I keep on crying, Uncle Joe will get tired of it.

She flipped the gilt-edged pages and saw tiny notes in the margins, in her mother's neat script. How many times had Sarah seen her bend over the book during church, adding a thought to the edge of a page, so she would remember it later? Watching her had planted the habit in Sarah, whose own Bible was beginning to fill up with handwritten notes about thoughts that struck her heart during church or devotions.

She saw a date inked beside a verse. Psalm 139:17. *How precious also are thy thoughts unto me, O God! how great is the sum of them!* The date was less than a month ago. Mom had read that verse and found it significant. Sarah thought about it. Yes, that would appeal to Mom. The majesty and value of God's Word. It was something they had talked about often as they read the Scripture together each morning over breakfast. She missed that.

Sarah determined at that moment that she would continue reading the Bible every day, even though Mom wasn't there to share her insights. She wondered what Uncle Joe would say if she suggested a time of devotions together every morning. Something told her he wasn't ready for that. For now, she would study on her own.

She placed her mother's Bible in the bookcase with her own paperbound copy and reached for the next box of treasures. As she arranged her ribbons and trophies on the second shelf, Uncle Joe came and stood in the doorway watching her.

"So what time do we go to church in the morning?" Sarah asked, shelving her horse books and back issues of *Horse & Rider*, her mother's birthday gift last year. She'd have to send a change of address card to the magazine.

Uncle Joe cleared his throat. "We'll leave around 9:30. I'll get up and feed. You don't have to get up 'til eight or so. Catch up on your sleep."

"No, I told you I'd take care of my own horses."

"Well, some days I might want you to feed my critters for me, so I'll just take a turn for you tomorrow."

Sarah hesitated, then said, "All right. Thank you." She wasn't sure she could sleep that late, knowing Uncle Joe would be up soon after dawn.

"You want to call your friends tonight?"

Sarah swallowed hard. "I don't want to be an expense to you."

"You can call." He ran a hand through his dark hair and leaned against the door jamb. "Mrs. Moseley made me promise to let you call once in a while."

Sarah stood up, wishing Uncle Joe would tell her how he felt about things, not just the basics of how things were. Was he glad she had friends who cared about her back home, or was it just one more detail that he had to remember and pay for?

She punched in the Moseleys' phone number, remembering to preface it with the northern California area code. When Aunt

Becky answered, the sound of her voice sent a shiver of homesickness through Sarah's stomach.

"I'm so glad you called, Sarah! We've been praying for you and wondering if you and your uncle got home all right."

"Yes, we're fine, and the horses did fine too."

"I'm glad. How do they like their new home?"

"Great. Uncle Joe has six other horses here right now, two of his, and four that he's training. Icicle and Clover are pretty excited about being with all of the others."

"I'll bet," said Aunt Becky. "Do you think you'll get along all right there?"

"Well, I guess so."

"Is anything wrong?" Aunt Becky's voice had a touch of concern.

"No, not really. Uncle Joe . . ."

"What, Sarah?"

She hesitated, not wanting to complain. "He doesn't talk much."

"I'm sorry, honey."

Sarah felt tears springing up in her eyes. Aunt Becky's tender tone reminded her too poignantly of her mother, and her eyes prickled.

"It's okay," she said. "I'm really glad he let me bring the horses."

"I am too. But you call me if anything goes wrong, you hear me? Or even if you just want to chat. You're like . . . well, almost like a daughter to me."

"I know. Thanks."

"I mean it, Sarah. If there's anything at all that you want to talk about, you call me."

"I will."

Eric came on the line then, and Sarah was buffeted by a fresh wave of longing.

"Sarah! I finally got to take Hannibal out for a good workout this morning. Have you ridden Icy yet?" he demanded.

"Yes, Uncle Joe and I rode this morning. He's got some great trails here. Not much woods, but there's one nice stretch with a bridge over a stream. I took Clover down there this afternoon too, just to give her a little exercise."

"Sounds like you've got some good places to ride."

"I think so. The neighbor lets me ride on his land too. I can go miles without crossing a road."

"I wish we could do that here. Sarah, are you going to be able to keep competing?"

She glanced around, but Uncle Joe had not followed her into the kitchen, so she felt secure in speaking frankly. "I don't know. We . . . we haven't talked about it really. My uncle's friend Junior says Uncle Joe's not much on competing, so I don't think he'll want to do it. I don't know if he'll let me anyway."

"But if you could get another sponsor—"

"I don't know, Eric," Sarah said, trying to hide her disappointment. "The ride is only three weeks away. You shouldn't plan on me being there."

"What about your uncle's friend?"

"Junior Tate? I thought of him, but I just don't know if he would do it or how to ask Uncle Joe."

"We'll pray about it."

"Thanks. If it seems right, I'll ask. But Uncle Joe is so quiet, it's kind of hard to know how much to say sometimes."

"We noticed that when he was here," Eric said. "My mom says he's about as noisy as a spider."

"Well, I guess I'd better go." She felt forlorn, and she was afraid she sounded that way too. Eric's voice was so normal, she wished she could go on listening to it. But she didn't want to run up a big phone bill for her uncle to pay, no matter what he had said.

"Sarah, we miss your mom too," Eric said softly.

"I know. Thanks."

"Does your uncle talk about her?"

"No."

"That's too bad. My mom says it helps to talk about the person that died, especially when it's someone you love."

She gulped. "Well, thanks. If I need someone to talk to, I'll call you and your mom, okay?"

"Sure."

She gave Eric the phone number and address for the ranch. "Now, you write to me, and I'll write to you, okay?"

"I'll do it tomorrow, after church," Eric promised. "Are you going to church up there?"

"Yes. I'm not sure what it will be like, but we're going."

5

The church wasn't like anything Sarah had ever known. The little weather-beaten building had no steeple. It stood alone on a rise in the plain, defying the wind that seemed to blow constantly. There was no sign and no parsonage nearby.

"Where does the pastor live?" she asked, as Uncle Joe pulled into the gravel yard and parked near two other pickups and a mini-van.

"About three miles north on Grindstone Road."

They got out, and Sarah followed him up the sagging steps to the church. The wind ruffled her hair, and she put her hand up nervously to brush her bangs into place. She had put on her best dress that morning. When she went to the kitchen to eat breakfast with Uncle Joe, she had immediately known she was overdressed.

Uncle Joe didn't own a suit. Sarah had learned that last week, when he arrived in California for her mother's funeral. His best outfit for summer seemed to be a clean white shirt, black pants, and a soft, dark leather vest. Sarah didn't think he owned a necktie either. She had made a quick decision and changed into a denim skirt and plaid blouse for church.

Uncle Joe wore his black Stetson as far as the church doorway, pulling it off as he crossed the threshold. Pastor Carleton and his wife greeted them and introduced Sarah to their college-age daughter and teenage son, Lissa and Matthew. Sarah wished they were younger. Matthew would be a high school senior this year, his mother revealed, and Lissa had been home for the summer, but would soon return to her college studies. Sarah wondered if she was the only ninth grader in Elk Creek.

Two other families filled the back pews on both sides of the aisle. Uncle Joe sat down in the next-to-last row. More people came in during the next ten minutes. Sarah saw Junior slip in just as the pastor opened Sunday school. He sat down on the other side of the aisle beside a middle-aged woman.

About forty people were squeezed into the little church by the time they broke up for classes. There were three Sunday school classes: adults, young people, and children.

Sarah leaned toward her uncle. "Am I a *young people*?" Her nerves were kicking up as she watched the children filing out a door beside the platform. Teenagers were going out through the front door.

"You can be if you want," he replied.

Sarah stared at him, perplexed.

Uncle Joe turned toward the aisle. "Hey, Skeeter!" he called softly.

A skinny, thirteen-year-old boy turned vivid blue eyes on him. "What's up, Joe?"

"Take my niece Sarah, here, with you."

It wasn't a question. Sarah got up and squeezed past Uncle Joe into the aisle.

"I'm Skeeter."

"Hi. I'm Sarah."

"I figured that out."

Sarah winced and followed the boy outside.

Matthew Carleton and two girls made up the rest of the class with her and Skeeter. A man of about forty was laying out his lesson book and some sheets of paper beside his Bible on the dry grass beyond the parking area.

"Do you always have Sunday school outside?" Sarah asked as they settled on the ground.

"Nah, not in the winter," Skeeter said. "We stay in with the old folks then. Don't have but one classroom. We need a bigger church."

"So why don't you build on?" Sarah asked.

"We're thinking about it."

The girl on the other side of him laughed. "Been thinking about it for fifty years."

Sarah looked at the red-haired girl, and immediately liked her. She wore a denim jumper over a green T-shirt, and scuffed brown boots. Her bright hair was cropped almost as short as Skeeter's, and her green eyes sparkled as she looked Sarah over.

The teacher was ready to open with prayer, so Sarah didn't say any more then, but when the lesson was over, she made sure the girl didn't get away.

"Hey, I'm Sarah Piper. What's your name?"

"Kayla Bergeron. You visiting Joe?"

"I'm going to live with him," Sarah said, watching Kayla's face.

"Oh, yeah? Cool. You like horses?"

"Yes. I brought mine with me."

"Yeah? What kind of horse?"

The two girls walked toward the church together. Skeeter, forgetting Sarah, charged on ahead with the other teenagers.

"Part quarter horse," Sarah said cautiously, but Kayla didn't laugh or ask her what the other part was.

"You going to school in Romney?"

Sarah swallowed. "I don't know yet. I never went to school before."

"Never?" Kayla's pale reddish eyebrows rose in incredulity.

"Nope. My mom taught me. I'm hoping Uncle Joe will teach me, but . . . well, I just don't know yet."

"Joe Piper's no teacher."

"No, but . . . well, he could do it if he wanted. He's smart."

Kayla cocked her head to one side. "Yeah, he's smart, but he's not a teacher."

"You don't have to be," Sarah insisted. "I've got my school books already. He'd just have to make sure I'm studying and tell the state."

"That doesn't sound right," said Kayla.

"Well, that's what we did back home."

"And you *never* went to school?" Kayla stopped in the church doorway, staring at her with those riveting green eyes.

"Nope. Never."

The red-haired girl hesitated, then asked, "Can you read?"

Sarah laughed. "Of course I can. My mom taught me when I was little."

Kayla shook her head. "Maybe I'll ride over and see you sometime."

"Sure. But Uncle Joe and I'll be gone tomorrow."

"I'll come Tuesday."

"All right. You got a horse?"

Kayla grinned. "Fastest thing you've ever seen."

"I doubt it," Sarah said with a smile. She slipped into the pew and sat beside Uncle Joe. He threw her a glance. Sarah thought he must have heard Kayla's last words in the aisle, when she said she would come over to visit, but Uncle Joe said nothing.

Once the worship service started, Sarah felt more at home. Although the church was small and unpainted and the pews were hard and uncomfortable, the spirit was the same. The people sang with feeling, and the pastor's message was straight from God's

Word. Sarah drew comfort from the knowledge that these people shared her faith.

After the service the pastor's wife came over to where they stood between the pews and held out her hand.

"So you're Joe's niece. Would that be on your father's side?"

"Yes, ma'am. My dad was Uncle Joe's brother."

"You must favor your mother then."

"People say I do." Sarah didn't add that, while her coloring was like her mother's, she despaired of ever being as pretty.

"You surely don't look like Joe."

Sarah smiled, ignoring the slight annoyance she felt. Everyone said the same thing. She looked at her uncle, who seemed half asleep. It was true her own light hair and blue eyes were a contrast to Uncle Joe's dark, wavy hair and brown eyes. He was tall too. Sarah's mother had stood five-foot-three, and Sarah was afraid she wouldn't surpass that by much.

"We're glad to have you here," said Mrs. Carleton.

"Thank you."

"I'm very sorry about your mother."

Sarah nodded, feeling a little uncomfortable. "I . . . thank you."

"If you need anything, you tell Pastor or me. That goes for you too," she added, turning her gaze on Uncle Joe.

He nodded, his eyes widening.

Mrs. Carleton held his look for a moment, then smiled. "I've raised two girls, so if you need any advice, give me a call, Joe Piper."

"Will do," Uncle Joe replied.

Mrs. Carleton turned away.

"Hey, Sarah!" Junior Tate was in the aisle. "How you doing, girl?"

"I'm good," Sarah replied.

"Glad to hear it. This here's Rose Zucker." Junior nodded toward the woman beside him.

The woman smiled at Sarah. "Pleased to meet a new neighbor."

Sarah nodded. "Hello."

Rose Zucker wasn't beautiful by any means, though her rounded face burst into a pleasant smile. She wore glasses, and her short, straight graying hair framed her tanned face. She must be as old as Grandma Anderson, Sarah thought.

Mrs. Zucker extended her hand. "I hear you're quite a horsewoman."

"Well . . ." Sarah could feel her cheeks flushing as she shook hands.

When Mrs. Zucker smiled, her warm, brown eyes lit behind the glasses, and she seemed almost pretty for a moment. Her purple blouse splashed bright next to Junior's white shirt, brightening the drab little church.

"Drop by and see me someday, Sarah."

"Thank you."

The woman's gaze flitted to Uncle Joe. "Morning, Joe."

Uncle Joe nodded.

"We're heading to the Carletons' for dinner," Junior said with a satisfied glance at Rose. "Are you two eating beans out of a can today?"

"Near enough," Uncle Joe said.

Sarah smiled. Another thing about Uncle Joe—he wasn't much for cooking, and Junior knew it.

They went out into the parking lot, and Sarah saw Kayla getting into a dusty station wagon with her parents and four younger, redheaded children. She waved, and Kayla waved back.

On the way home Sarah ventured, "That Mrs. Zucker seems nice."

"I s'pose."

"What happened to Mr. Zucker, if I'm allowed to ask?"

Uncle Joe's lips twitched, and she thought for a moment he wouldn't answer, but then he said, "About ten years ago, he tried to herd an Angus bull in from the pasture on foot and got himself trampled to death."

Sarah swallowed hard, not liking that image. She stared out the window trying to think of another topic. Her stomach rumbled.

"What *are* we going to eat?" she asked. They'd had sandwiches twice the day before.

"Hadn't thought much about it."

"Well, hey, I can cook something," she offered.

Uncle Joe eyed her with speculation. "Should I be happy or insulted?"

Was there a twinkle in his eyes? Sarah laughed. "What have you got in the house?"

"Not much. I expect I need to shop on the way home from Salem tomorrow."

Sarah inventoried the pantry and made scrambled eggs, sausage, and fried potatoes for lunch, plenty of it.

"Not bad atall," Uncle Joe murmured after two bites. That was all he said until the food was gone.

When they had finished, however, he surveyed all the dirty dishes with an injured air. "One bad thing about cooking," he said.

Sarah winced. "Yes, sir." She carried her place setting to the sink and began running hot water.

To her surprise Uncle Joe opened a drawer and brought out a dish towel.

"What?" he asked, meeting Sarah's stare.

"Nothing." She turned back to the sink and began plunking dishes in the hot water. He kept up with her, drying the dishes and putting them away.

"So when we're shipshape, you want to take those nags out again?" he asked.

"I'd like to."

"I ought to take Zorro out. He's probably full of kinks, just sitting around doing nothing for a solid week. Ranger too."

"I'd like to learn more trails," Sarah said. "I have to put a lot of miles on Icy and Clover."

Uncle Joe carefully dried the deep bowl Sarah had scrambled the eggs in.

"When were you supposed to ride again?"

"Compete, you mean?"

He nodded.

Sarah plunged her hands into the warm water, searching for the dishrag, hardly daring to hope he was interested. "Well, we signed up for the Bandicoot 100. That's three weeks from now, the twenty-sixth. But . . ." She let it trail off.

Uncle Joe went on drying dishes.

Sarah dredged the last of the silverware out of the water, rinsed it, and handed it to him, then let the water drain out of the sink.

"Get changed," he said. "We need to get moving."

6

When Sarah came out of the bedroom in her jeans, the house was empty, and she hurried to the barn. Uncle Joe had Zorro saddled and was putting his bridle on him. Sarah seized Icicle's tack and went to his stall. When she led the gelding out, Uncle Joe was mounting in the barnyard.

"Is it okay to just leave everything open?" Sarah asked as she pulled herself into the saddle. She and her mother had always locked the house and stable when they went out to ride for several hours.

"It's fine." Uncle Joe wheeled Zorro, and Sarah didn't have to urge the gray to follow. Icicle was frisky, eager to run with the big black.

"You gotta pace him," Uncle Joe said.

"Yes, sir. We mostly trot on long rides."

He said no more, but led her on an extended ramble, over hills, through dry ravines, and along a dirt road for two miles. They cut off across a stretch of sagebrush, and far ahead Sarah could see mountains.

Uncle Joe pointed toward the highest peak. "If you go a couple of miles that way, you'll come to lava beds," he said. "It's real hard on the horses' feet."

Sarah nodded soberly. She would remember. She wasn't used to the openness of the landscape, being able to see miles ahead. At home they had ridden through forest and along the edges of farmland. It was exciting to be on the range, miles from the nearest house, but it made her feel vulnerable, and she was glad Uncle Joe was with her.

Soon he veered to the left and dismounted to open a wire gate. They led the horses through it, and he hooked the two strands of wire again.

"Is this part of Junior's?" Sarah asked.

"Nope. It's Eldon Smith's range. He doesn't care if you ride here. There's a cattle guard on the far side. Not a gate, just a grating on the ground."

Sarah nodded. She had seen one before.

They rode around the edge of the fenced range. A small herd of Herefords stopped grazing to eye them dolefully, then went back to nibbling the dry grass.

"I'll have to show you on a map, so you can get it in your head," Uncle Joe said, when they came to the cattle guard.

Sarah looked at her watch. "How far have we come, Uncle Joe?"

"Nigh on five miles, I guess." He walked Zorro through the opening in the fence, and Sarah followed on Icicle.

The next stretch, after they had crossed a paved road, was in the foothills. It was rugged terrain, but Sarah was glad, as she knew Icicle needed to practice all kinds of footing. As they gained altitude, they entered a forest of noble fir, ponderosa, and jack pine.

"You might see a deer or a herd of elk up here."

"Yes, sir."

He looked at her sideways.

"Sorry. I mean, Uncle Joe."

He pulled his battered black Stetson off and mopped his forehead with his sleeve. "You can just call me Joe."

Sarah bit her lip. Her mother's training wouldn't allow that. "No, I don't think I can, if it's all the same to you—" She bit back the *sir* at the last moment.

"Make me feel old," he muttered.

"Sorry."

This wasn't going well. Sarah was beginning to feel she was a weight around Uncle Joe's neck. If the man had wanted children, he would have married years ago.

He glanced at her, then looked off toward the horizon. "Well, look, I'll take you back by way of Black Peter Bridge. That'll be ten or twelve miles by the time we're done."

Sarah nodded. "Thanks."

"Is that a decent ride for that horse?"

"Yes—well, it's a pretty good workout. Sometimes we used to take them out longer, but . . . well, I probably don't need to now."

"You mean, 'cause they're in shape?"

"No, s—no. I just . . ." Sarah felt a little sick with nervousness. She wanted to discuss competing, but not if Uncle Joe would forbid it. "Well, if they're not going to compete, they don't need so much training is all." She had to face it. If he wasn't willing, she would have to give it up, and she might as well ease off on the long rides.

He said nothing more, and Sarah felt a great sadness well up within her heart. It wasn't the competition. It was seeing the end of what she and her mother had loved, the one thing they had excelled at together. Mom's face was always so joyful and eager on the morning of a big ride. She knew, she just knew they would finish, and place well to boot. Sarah could only remember one ride where they hadn't finished together. It was the last one she had taken old Chester to.

Her father's horse, Chester, was well past his prime when Sarah started taking him on endurance rides, and by the time Icicle was old enough and trained, Chester was ready to retire. That last fifty-mile ride had been too much for the old gelding. He had gone lame eight miles from the finish, and Sarah had walked into the next-to-last vet check leading him. After the horse had been examined and disqualified, Sarah had encouraged her mother to go on without her, to finish with Clover. Sarah couldn't go on alone, but Mom could.

But her mother had refused. They saw Aunt Becky and Eric off on that final leg of the race, then loaded their mounts in a trailer provided by the sponsoring association and rode to the finish line in the truck. It had been a disappointment, the end of a series of happy times for the four of them.

Sarah knew Chester wouldn't compete again, and she wouldn't either until the next spring when Icicle would be old enough to qualify. Putting her father's horse out to pasture had been hard for her and her mother, and it was hard on Chester too. The old gelding died that winter.

Riding Icicle had been the beginning of new adventures. The spirited young gray had already won Sarah's heart. She had ridden him at home, long before he was mature enough for the endurance rides. She did everything for Icicle—fed him, groomed him, kept his stall clean. Icy was the first horse that was truly her own.

Sarah had anticipated the Bandicoot with the feeling that this would be the big test for her and Icicle, to prove their maturity and their stamina. Now that hope was dashed.

As they rode toward Black Peter Bridge, she forgot to take note of the landmarks for future reference. Instead, she was thinking about her mother, and wondering if she really wanted to compete without her, after all. Would she feel all empty because her mom wasn't there? Or would she still be happy, knowing Mom had loved the sport, and knowing she would want Sarah to go on, even when she was exhausted, even when her heart ached?

Sarah doubted she could ever feel as close to Uncle Joe as she had to Mom, but still, sharing the challenging experience of the ride might help them overcome the invisible wall between them. It was too confusing, and she slumped in the saddle, letting Icicle jog along behind Zorro, lengthening his stride now and then to keep up.

Icicle was a big horse, over sixteen hands, but Zorro was an inch taller, and his stride was longer. It ate up the trail effortlessly. Unlike wiry little Clover, who jogged steadily along with an economy of movement, the long-legged black stretched out in fluid motion. Icicle fell somewhere in between, tall and fast, but a little more fretful than Zorro. He tossed his head and sniffed the wind, testing the new smells that came to him, and he broke into a sweat before the black did. Once he was used to the territory and the other horses, Sarah was sure Icicle would be as calm and steady as Zorro.

At Black Peter Bridge Uncle Joe halted, dismounted, and showed Sarah where to lead her horse down to the stream for a drink. They rested for fifteen minutes on the bank and let the horses crop the grass that was still green near the water.

Sarah roused herself to pay more attention on the placid ride back to the ranch, but the melancholy stayed with her. The sun was sinking toward the horizon when they rode into the barnyard, and they tended their mounts before bringing in the other horses and feeding them all.

She spent an extra few minutes brushing Icicle as the horse ate his ration of grain. Uncle Joe was a good man she was sure, but he wasn't much for talking, and he wasn't much for children—of that Sarah was now certain. With Eric seven long hours away by car, Icicle was the staunchest friend she had left.

7

The long ride to Salem was very quiet. Sarah couldn't help contrasting it mentally with the trips she and her mother had made, hauling their horses to rides. They had talked and planned and laughed, even sung together on the way, silly, boisterous songs and quiet hymns.

Uncle Joe, on the other hand, spoke once in the first two hours. Sarah thought about bringing up the subject of school while she had him captive in the cab of the pickup, but decided against that. Maybe if she didn't mention it, he would never get around to talking about it. As long as they didn't talk about it, she could always hope she wouldn't have to go to school.

She fought down the sense of loneliness that engulfed her. God was with her every step of the way, she knew that. As they drove the winding road over the Cascade Mountains, she thrilled at the views that opened one after the other before her. The Bible passage she had read that morning came to her mind. "Lift up your eyes on high, and behold who hath created these things" (Isaiah 40:26). Yes, the evidence of God's power was all around her, and she would wait to see what He would do in her life.

Dulcet whinnied as they headed down a steep grade, and Uncle Joe frowned, watching the rearview mirror.

"We'll pull over as soon as we can and give her a little break. It's hard on a horse, having to brace on these turns and inclines."

Sarah nodded. She was thankful for even that little insight Uncle Joe had shared. *In time,* she thought. *In God's time, we'll grow closer, and he'll teach me.* She sent up a silent prayer. *Thank you, Lord, for putting me with Uncle Joe. If I can't have Mom anymore, there's no one else I'd rather be with.*

When at last they reached the home of Dulcet's owner, Sarah sprang out of the truck and watched Uncle Joe unload the Arabian in front of the barn. It was a low, modern stable that looked new, with a phone and a kitchenette inside the door, next to the tack room. The nearby house was constructed of irregular granite blocks, with a glass wall fronting the living room and shrubs and perennial beds all around. Pop-up sprinklers kept roses and snapdragons blooming in the driest of the Oregon dry season. Dulcet lifted her head and gave a shrill neigh.

Mrs. Randolph stood by in riding breeches and boots, the shiny black English kind. Sarah supposed she showed her horses in both English and Western classes at the horse shows. She was perhaps forty years old, Sarah guessed, but it was hard to tell. Her hair was so blonde it was nearly white, but her eyebrows were dark, and she wore lipstick and mascara, a funny getup for riding, Sarah thought.

"Dulcet is doing well," Uncle Joe said, leading the mare over to stand before the woman, and Sarah could have shaken him. It was the understatement of the year. The horse behaved perfectly, and he ought to praise her more to the owner.

"What about the bridges?"

"No problem now. Just head her right at it and be confident."

"Are you sure? Because I've entered her in a largish show for next week, and I don't want to be embarrassed."

"Well, ma'am, if you do what I say and don't hesitate, she won't either." Uncle Joe pulled his hat off and scratched his head. "You got a practice bridge?"

"No, I think that was part of the problem. She hadn't practiced enough."

"Well, if you had a place where I could demonstrate . . ."

"The closest bridge is two miles away, I'm afraid."

"You want to take her over there?"

"Oh, no, that's too much trouble."

"No, ma'am. This is important to you. I think it might be worth it if we took Dulcet to a bridge right now and had you take her over it," Uncle Joe persisted.

Mrs. Randolph looked uneasy. "She nearly threw me the last time, you know."

"She won't today. Tell you what, let me put her back in the trailer, and you climb in. It will only take a few minutes, and you'll be a lot happier, once you see her perform."

"Well . . . all right." She smiled tentatively, and Uncle Joe nodded. He led Dulcet back toward the ramp of the trailer.

The mare hesitated, as though she would balk at entering the contraption again, but Uncle Joe leaned on the halter a little.

"Up, girl."

Dulcet put one hoof on the ramp, then another and meekly kept walking beside him.

When he emerged, he leaned close to Sarah and whispered, "You get in the other side of the trailer."

Sarah stared at him. She wasn't allowed to ride in trailers. She started to open her mouth, then closed it. Maybe he didn't want the sophisticated Mrs. Randolph sitting practically in his lap in the front of the truck.

He looked over at the owner and nodded toward the pickup. "Hop in, ma'am."

"What about your daughter?"

Uncle Joe sighed. "She's not my kid."

"Oh, I'm sorry."

Sarah felt her cheeks go scarlet. If only Uncle Joe had added, "She's my niece." She felt as though she had been disowned.

"You getting in?" he asked sharply, glancing at Sarah.

"Oh, well, yes," said Mrs. Randolph.

"Not you, ma'am, sorry."

"Oh." She looked at him, then at Sarah. "The girl can ride up here with us."

"I could just wait here," Sarah said.

Uncle Joe frowned at her. "Forget that notion. Get in the truck." He heaved the ramp up as Sarah stepped away, and Dulcet jumped when it hit the back of the trailer.

Sarah had never seen her uncle so unsettled, and she tried not to take offense at his curtness. Mrs. Randolph made him nervous, Sarah was sure, and he didn't want to drive off alone with her, leaving Sarah behind.

The woman opened the pickup door and waited, conveying to Sarah without words that she was to sit in the middle, which was probably a good thing. It was the only solution that would leave Uncle Joe calm enough to drive safely.

Sarah climbed in, trying not to lean against either of them as her uncle maneuvered the turns in the road. Mrs. Randolph directed him to a quiet little dirt lane that ran alongside a field of fragrant spearmint.

When they were within sight of the bridge, a wooden structure with sides three feet high, he pulled to the side of the road against a high dirt bank and went to unload the mare again. Mrs. Randolph opened the door and climbed down.

"Ma'am," Sarah said as she got out.

"Yes?" The woman turned toward her expectantly.

"He's my uncle, ma'am."

"Oh. I thought maybe you worked for him, and I upset him when I said what I did."

"No, ma'am. I think he didn't like it because it makes him feel old for you to think I'm his daughter."

"I see. Should I—"

"No, ma'am, I don't think so. Best leave it alone."

Mrs. Randolph smiled a little and nodded. She wasn't so stuck up after all, Sarah thought, and she decided to put in a plug for Uncle Joe.

"He's the best trainer there is, ma'am."

"So I was told. I guess we'll find out now."

Mrs. Randolph walked around to where he had tied the mare to the back of the trailer and was saddling her. When Dulcet was ready, he unhooked the chain from her halter, led her a few paces from the rig, and mounted.

"Now, you just watch, ma'am." He urged Dulcet into an even jog, headed for the exact center of the bridge. Below it, the water tumbled over stones, swishing and swirling. As she approached the bridge, the mare swung her head a little, but Uncle Joe checked her movements and pushed her forward. She shivered, but didn't falter when her hooves hit the first timber. He took her calmly over the bridge and a few paces beyond, then turned her and came back toward them at the same measured, quiet gait.

Sarah looked at Mrs. Randolph then, and the woman's eyes were shining.

"I can't believe it! She never used to want to go near it. She'd hear the water and get all upset, and when she got to the bridge she'd go crazy."

"My Uncle Joe is the best," Sarah repeated. The pride that swelled in her chest amazed and pleased her. If he was embarrassed to claim her, she would work her hardest to change that, because she wanted to claim him.

"But will she do it for me?"

Sarah realized that Mrs. Randolph was wary, still a little frightened from her previous scare.

"Whoa," Uncle Joe said as the mare came even with them, in a voice so low Sarah could barely hear it, but Dulcet stopped in her tracks, and Uncle Joe swung down in one easy motion.

"Your turn." He held the reins out to Mrs. Randolph.

"Do you think—?"

"It's not what I think, it's what you think," Uncle Joe said. "If you're sure you're going over that bridge, then you are. Don't for a second let this animal think you're not."

Mrs. Randolph looked at him for a long moment, then nodded with resolution and stepped forward, putting her left foot high up to the stirrup. Sarah wondered if Uncle Joe would reach out and give her a boost, but he didn't. When Mrs. Randolph was in the saddle though, he went around and adjusted the right stirrup while she pulled up the leather on the left.

"All right." Mrs. Randolph gathered the reins and squared her shoulders. "Let's go, girl."

Dulcet started forward at a walk.

"Put your legs into her," Uncle Joe said, and Sarah thought there was a touch of despair in his tone.

Just before the bridge, Dulcet checked, but Mrs. Randolph responded firmly. "Come on!"

Sarah could see that she was using her legs to push the mare forward. Dulcet tossed her head and stepped onto the bridge. Mrs. Randolph said, "That's it, keep going," and they did.

Sarah grinned and looked at her uncle as Dulcet approached the far side of the stream. His face was far from jubilant.

"Flighty doesn't inspire confidence in a horse," he muttered.

"She's pretty," Sarah offered.

"Huh." Uncle Joe shook his head. "Pretty out of a bottle." His eyes never left Dulcet as Mrs. Randolph turned her around and headed her back toward the bridge. This time the mare did not hesitate, but stepped without a shudder onto the planks.

Mrs. Randolph was laughing when she reached them. "I still don't believe it! Thank you! She's never been so obedient for me!"

Uncle Joe's eyes still held a dubious flicker. "Well, ma'am, you've got to be steady and calm. Practice a lot. If there are other bridges you can try, do it, so she'll be used to lots of different situations. But mostly it's your commitment that counts. You can't ever believe this horse is going to balk, because she'll know it, and she will do it. Do you get what I'm saying?"

"I . . . I think so." She eyed him uncertainly. "I think you're saying a good rider can make this horse do anything."

"Well . . . yes, ma'am, I think so. No offense intended. She's a really smart horse."

Mrs. Randolph nodded. "Perhaps I'm the one who needs more training, so I can help Dulcet reach her potential."

She swung lightly to the ground, passing the reins to him, and he hooked the horse to the trailer. Sarah had the saddle off before he could get back there, and she lugged it to the back of the truck while he unbridled the mare.

Back at the house, Dulcet once more came down the ramp and was led into her stall, where she was given a generous dinner of oats, a bucket of water, and some carrots.

"And now, Mr. Piper, if you'll step into the house for a moment, I'll get your check," Mrs. Randolph said with a grand sweep of her arm toward the front door. "Oh, and your niece can help herself to a bottle of soda if you don't mind, right there in the refrigerator." She nodded toward the little kitchen in the barn.

"Thank you," Sarah said, watching Uncle Joe. He nodded at her.

Mrs. Randolph smiled at her and walked toward her house. Uncle Joe hung back, then followed her with his shoulders slumped, and Sarah realized this was a difficult part of the business for him, accepting his compensation. Was it timidity? Or pride? Maybe he just wasn't comfortable with women. But, no, Sarah thought he wouldn't have felt any easier if it were Mr. Randolph handing over the fee. Uncle Joe always seemed a lot more comfortable with horses than he did with humans.

He hesitated at the door of the house, then followed Mrs. Randolph inside. Sarah strolled to the compact refrigerator and looked over the selection of soft drinks.

8

Sarah waited beside the truck and sipped her cola until Uncle Joe came out of the house, stuffing something into his shirt pocket, and climbed into the driver's seat. She scrambled in on the passenger side.

"You hungry?" he asked as he started the engine.

"Yes."

"We'd best get something to eat before we pick up the next horse."

"Next horse?" Sarah was startled.

Uncle Joe kept his eyes on the road. "I was supposed to pick up a horse last Thursday, but I called and told the owner I couldn't get him until today."

Sarah let that sink in. "Because you were helping me." And with her two horses in his barn, he wouldn't have had room for another client's horse, she realized. "Uncle Joe, Clover and Icicle can stay outside all night if you need the space. I don't want you to lose money because of me."

"Don't fret about it. If I need the space, I'll tell you."

He drove toward town and pulled into a parking lot near a fast food restaurant, parking the truck and trailer at the far edge of the lot out of the way of other vehicles.

"Come on, let's have a burger."

Sarah followed him inside. They each ate two burgers, a mountain of fries, large drinks, and dessert.

Back on the road, Sarah was sleepy, but guilt nagged at her too.

"Uncle Joe," she said at last, "you're paying for my food and everything now, aren't you?"

"I told you not to fret."

"Maybe you just can't afford me."

He laughed then. "Sarah, I don't ever want to hear that again. You're my brother's daughter."

She looked ahead at the rolling hills. A vast herd of Herefords covered the pasture they were passing. She couldn't forget how he'd said testily to Mrs. Randolph, "She's not my kid."

"Uncle Joe, you're supposed to use what money my mom had to take care of me. Isn't that what the lawyer told you?"

"Aw, Sarah, there's not enough to amount to a hill of beans, if you want the truth. We'll put it in the bank, and if you want to go to college some day, it will be a start. Meanwhile, I guess I can scrape up enough to feed one stringy little beanpole and a couple of flea-bitten nags."

"You did love my dad, didn't you?" she asked, suddenly unsure that Uncle Joe had ever loved anyone except horses. "I mean, is that why you're keeping me?"

"Aw, Sarah," he said again, then he was quiet.

It was nearly an hour before they came to the home of the new horse's owner. This one was a bay quarter horse gelding nicknamed Buzz. The sixteen-year-old girl who owned him wanted Uncle Joe to train him for western equitation. Sarah surmised that her daddy was paying the bill. He hovered in the barnyard while his daughter got ready to bring the horse out, laughing and talking loudly to

Uncle Joe about the cost of keeping horseflesh and how teenaged girls found horse shows monumental.

The girl fussed over Buzz and hugged and kissed him before they loaded him, cooing over him and admonishing Uncle Joe to take good care of him.

"Nothing but the best," he assured her.

The girl, her father, and her older brother pushed Buzz into the trailer while Uncle Joe pulled. The horse balked, but relented when Uncle Joe held a little grain under his nose.

Once they were on the road again, Sarah settled down, expecting another long, silent ride, but Uncle Joe surprised her.

"Sarah, don't you worry none about where your feed's coming from, you hear me?"

"Yes, sir."

"Just because I don't have much food in the house doesn't mean I'm broke, okay?"

Sarah looked down at her hands, embarrassed. "Okay."

"I just don't hoard food is all."

"All right." She glanced toward him, but he was watching the road.

"This check I got from Mrs. Randolph today will feed you and me and all the horses for a good, long time," he said. "You get what I'm saying?"

"Yes. Yes, I do."

He smiled then. "Good. And one more thing."

Sarah arched her eyebrows in question.

"I got a little exasperated back there at Randolphs', but it wasn't at you."

"It wasn't?"

"Nope."

Sarah felt better then. It wasn't much, but it made a warm spot inside her, and she thought that, with time and care, Uncle Joe might learn to love and to let someone know it. She closed her eyes and thanked God for her uncle and her new home, and asked Him to take away the ache that was there where her mother's love had been.

She jerked awake several hours later. "Where are we?"

"Romney. Almost home."

She stretched her arms. "I guess I was out."

"Like a light. Listen, I'm going in the store, and I may be a few minutes. There's a little bank in there, and I can get rid of this check and pick up some vittles."

Sarah smiled. "My favorite."

"Huh! Well, you stay put with the horse, okay?"

"Sure."

"Anything special you want me to get?"

"How about some pancake mix and syrup?"

"Sure thing." He paused for a second, then looked toward the store. "Any girl stuff?"

Sarah felt her cheeks flush. "No, but thanks for asking."

It was half an hour before he reappeared with a grocery cart piled high with plastic grocery bags. Sarah got out and helped him heft them into the back of the truck. Buzz whinnied and pawed in the trailer.

"Looks like we'll be eating well now," Sarah commented. She could see bananas, crackers, and a tray of chicken breasts poking from the tops of bags.

"Ought to last a couple of days," Uncle Joe said, and she smiled.

When they got home, he turned Buzz in to Dulcet's empty stall. Sarah began the routine of evening feeding, measuring out the rations into each horse's feed box. When they were done, they went to the pasture gate and brought the other horses in. Icicle rubbed his head against Sarah's shoulder, and she leaned back against him. When she had put the gray in his stall, she went for a soft brush. Stroking the big animal's sleek, warm coat was a comfort. She had thought the girl who owned Buzz was overly sentimental when she hugged Buzz fiercely and kissed his nose, but maybe it wasn't so silly, after all.

"You coming in?" Uncle Joe asked, leaning on the stall door.

"Sure."

She left the stall and latched the door, depositing the brush in its place on the way out of the barn. Uncle Joe shut the barn door, and they drove up to the house and unpacked their groceries.

"Doughnuts! You bought doughnuts?" It surprised her.

"For tomorrow," he said.

Sarah was puzzled.

"When that ornery, red-headed girl shows up."

"You mean Kayla?"

He grunted.

"You don't like her, do you?"

"Aw, she's a good kid. A little undisciplined."

"I should have asked you first if I could invite her over, but I thought you heard." Sarah stopped. "I guess I'm a little bit confused, Uncle Joe."

"About what?" He opened a crock and plunked a ten-pound bag of flour into it.

"Are you a parent or a friend or what? To me, I mean."

Uncle Joe sighed. "Well, I guess . . . I'll try to be both of those, Sarah, but I'm not sure I'm good at being either. Got no experience in the parent department, and . . . well, you've seen what kind of friends I collect."

"I like Junior," she said.

"You've got no taste." He shook his head and pulled several cans from a paper sack. "I'm your guardian now, Sarah, but I'm not sure what guardians are supposed to do."

Sarah felt she had a chance to begin building something good for both of them, and she took a deep breath. "Well, so far, you're doing pretty well, I think."

"That so?" He looked doubtful.

"Yes, sir. I mean, Uncle Joe. You didn't have to take me."

He looked off out the window, into the twilight. "Guess not. Not exactly. But I wanted to for some reason."

She stepped closer and touched his sleeve, and he looked down into her eyes.

"I'm glad you did, Uncle Joe." Her voice caught, as she thought about how miserable she would be if he had left California without offering her and the horses a home.

He nodded a little, looking uncomfortable. "So . . . we eating pancakes tonight?"

"You bet. The best pancakes you ever ate."

9

Tuesday morning Sarah rose early and went through the barn routine with Uncle Joe. She watched him pour Buzz's grain ration on the ramp of the horse trailer.

"Why are you feeding him out here?" she asked.

"That bonehead needs a lesson on trailering. I'll feed him on the ramp for a couple of days, then start putting it in the trailer."

"What if he won't go in the trailer for it?" Sarah asked.

"Then he won't eat. But he'll go in. Pretty soon he'll think that trailer is a gourmet restaurant."

Uncle Joe worked with Buzz while Sarah shoveled manure. When all the stalls were clean, she started spreading pine shavings in each enclosure. She was doing Ranger's stall when Uncle Joe returned to the barn after putting the bay out to pasture.

"Hey, you've got no call to muck out my horses," he said sharply.

"It's okay, I don't mind." Sarah leaned on her shovel. "If I do this, you'll have more time to work the horses."

Uncle Joe stood thinking. "You taking your gray out today?"

"Thought I would."

"Well, if Kayla shows up this morning, you can have some fun, then later, whatever critters need exercise, we'll have a ride up to Borden Corners. That's a good ride. Seven miles from here."

Sarah nodded. "Is that girl coming today for her lesson?"

"Nope. Tomorrow. Wednesday and Saturday her daddy brings her."

Outside, the horses began to neigh and tear back and forth along the pasture fence.

"Sounds like company." Uncle Joe strode toward the barn door, and Sarah followed him outside.

Kayla Bergeron was riding up the driveway at an easy canter astride a flashy Appaloosa. The gelding's front quarters were a dark gray, but somewhere under the saddle a pure white blanket began, and over his hindquarters the white was dotted with black spots. The black mane and tail floated in the breeze of his speed.

Sarah couldn't help grinning. "Nice horse."

"Yup, if that girl doesn't ruin him."

Kayla pulled up hard before them, and the Appaloosa reared, pawed with his front feet, then plopped back down on all fours.

Uncle Joe shook his head and turned back toward the dim interior of the barn. "Lunch at noon. Be here."

"Yes, sir." Sarah stepped forward. "Howdy, Kayla."

"Howdy yourself."

"What's your horse's name?"

"Cracker. You got something to ride?"

Sarah went to the pasture gate. She didn't have to whistle. Icicle was there, waiting expectantly, whickering deep in his throat. It was difficult to get him out without letting any of the other horses through the gate, but Sarah managed. She led Icy into the barn and put him in the first set of cross ties. As she went for the saddle, Kayla appeared in the doorway on foot, holding the reins of the Appaloosa's bridle behind her. Farther down the barn aisle, Uncle Joe was saddling Jackson, the palomino gelding.

66

Kayla appraised Icicle, looking over his long legs and deep chest.

"He's big," she said at last. "Can he run?"

"Sure."

"Wanna race?"

"I'd have to warm him up first."

When Sarah went for the bridle, Uncle Joe came up behind her and put his hand on her shoulder. Sarah looked up at him in surprise.

"Just remember," he said quietly, "that horse of yours is a valuable animal. You're depending on him staying healthy. Don't take any foolish chances with him because some young daredevil is egging you on."

Sarah nodded. "I'll remember."

He went back to Jackson and unhooked the snaps of the cross ties. Sarah quickly bridled Icicle, and the two led their mounts outside.

"That's a good-looking horse," Kayla said, eyeing the palomino. "Can he run?"

"Well, I never clocked him."

Uncle Joe swung into the saddle and walked Jackson toward the training ring without looking back.

"Your uncle doesn't talk much," Kayla observed.

"Not much for words," Sarah agreed with a wry smile.

The girls walked their horses down the driveway and along the edge of the road for half a mile, then Kayla turned off into a broad expanse of grass and low brush. It was already hot. They jogged along for a ways, then Kayla waved her arm toward a rise ahead of them, where a lone cottonwood tree stood silhouetted against the cloudless sky.

"See that tree?"

"Yup."

"Race you," said Kayla, gathering her reins.

"Wait!" Sarah cried.

"What?" The Appaloosa had already bunched his hindquarters to spring into a gallop. Kayla pulled him up.

"Do you ride here a lot? Is it safe?"

"Sure, it's safe."

"No holes or anything?"

"Nope. Well, there's a gully over yonder." Kayla pointed to the left, and Sarah could see where the ground dropped.

"How about chuckholes?"

"Nope."

"Okay. Ready?"

"Ready." Kayla positioned herself low in the saddle.

Sarah gathered Icicle beneath her.

"Go!" Kayla shouted.

The horses streaked across the field. Icicle stuck close to Cracker's rump at first, his black hooves pounding on the turf. Sarah edged him up beside the Appaloosa, and Kayla threw her a gleeful glance and laid into Cracker with her boot heels.

Sarah didn't kick her horse, she just squeezed him a little and clucked once. Icicle strained forward, his ears flat, creeping up bit by bit. Sarah tried to watch the ground ahead of them, still not confident to be taking unfamiliar turf at such a breakneck pace.

They reach the tree together, and Icicle plunged past it a few yards before Sarah pulled him in a circle to join Kayla and Cracker in the poplar's shade on the west side of the tree.

"Was he flat out?" Kayla asked, grinning.

"I don't think so."

"He's not half bad," Kayla conceded, shoving her short bangs back with her fingers.

"Yeah, well, if you really wanted a race, I think there's a better horse in Uncle Joe's barn," Sarah admitted.

"That so?"

"His black horse, Zorro. We rode together the other day, and that horse can go. We didn't run them much, but just from the way he moves, I'd say he's the one to challenge."

"Does Joe let you ride him?"

"Not yet. I've got enough horses of my own to ride anyway."

"How many?"

"Two. But I have to put the miles on them."

"How come? They aren't race horses."

"Endurance horses. We go for mileage, not speed."

"You compete?"

"Yeah."

"Wow." Kayla watched her with new respect. "When's your next ride?"

Sarah hesitated. "Well, we're entered in one the twenty-sixth."

"You and Joe?"

"No, I meant me and Icicle."

"Oh. Whereabouts?"

"It's the Bandicoot 100. Ever hear of it?"

"Sure." Kayla patted Cracker's neck. "It's named for some famous horse, isn't it?"

Sarah nodded. "It starts over at John Day."

"I'll bet Cracker could do it."

"I don't know," Sarah countered. "You have to train pretty hard."

"You ride him every day?" Kayla asked, looking critically at Icicle.

"Not every day. Most days. I like to take him ten or twelve miles a day. Once a week I'll try to make a longer ride, twenty miles or so. If things work out for the Bandicoot, I'll need to take him on a thirty- or forty-mile ride next week to prepare him for it. But I'm just getting to know the trails around here. Uncle Joe's been showing me where I can ride."

Kayla nodded thoughtfully. "Well, my pa won't care if you ride over our way. Want to go over there now, so you'll know the way? You can get there without riding on paved roads at all, just cross the Romney Road once."

"Sure. How far is it?"

"Another three miles from here maybe."

"Let's go."

On the way the girls planned to meet the next day at Kayla's house. Sarah figured that a four-mile ride each way to Bergerons' plus a few miles with Kayla once she got there would be a good workout for either of her horses. She would clear it with Uncle Joe when she got home.

At Kayla's house they tied the horses to a hitching post in the front yard, and Kayla led Sarah in through the back door. Mrs. Bergeron stood at the sink wearing an apron. Dishes and cooking utensils spread out over the counter. The kitchen smelled good—baking grain and sugar scents.

"Well, hello. You're Sarah Piper."

"Yes, ma'am."

Mrs. Bergeron's hair was a dull brown, and Sarah knew the children got their fiery hair from their father. Her face was lined but peaceful.

A seven-year-old girl with coppery braids stared up at Sarah. "Are you a bachelor like Mr. Piper?"

Sarah laughed. "I don't think so."

"She's a spinster, Trudy," Kayla said. "Got any cookies, Mom?"

Mrs. Bergeron opened her oven door, and a wonderful fragrance bathed them. "It just so happens, I do. You came at the right time."

The girls ate several chocolate chip cookies and drank cold milk.

"Kayla tells me you don't go to school," Mrs. Bergeron said, stirring a smooth batter in her thick pottery mixing bowl.

"No, ma'am, I've been taught at home."

"Is Joe going to teach you now?"

"We're not sure yet." Sarah didn't like thinking about it.

"If you go to Romney, we'll ride the bus together," Kayla said.

"What time does the bus come?"

"About seven."

"Seven? That's early." Sarah began figuring mentally what time she would have to get up to feed the horses and clean the stalls, then wash up before the bus came.

Mrs. Bergeron poured the batter into a rectangular pan and scraped the bowl. "Well, it takes awhile to pick up all the kids, they're so scattered. You'd be about an hour on the bus, I guess."

Sarah didn't like the sound of that. She would lose an hour, morning and afternoon, just riding a pokey old school bus. Maybe she could study on the way home. But still, she'd be away from the ranch from seven in the morning until four o'clock or so in the afternoon.

"Come on," Kayla said, carrying their glasses to the counter. "I'll show you my new school clothes."

Sarah followed her down a hallway and into a large bedroom. It was crammed with furniture: a single bed, a set of bunks, two night-stands, three dressers, a bookcase, a desk, and two chairs. Clothes spilled out of the dresser drawers, and the closet door stood half open.

Kayla scowled. "Sorry it's a mess. That's what happens when you have to fight for your space."

"You share your room?"

"Yeah, with Trudy and Rachel. What a pain."

"I don't know. It must be fun to have sisters."

"Fun?" Kayla turned her eyes to the ceiling. "That's not the word I would have chosen." She swung the closet door wide and shoved several hanging garments aside. "Mom made me get one skirt, so this is my dressy outfit. Mostly I wear pants to school."

Sarah reached for the hanger and felt the swishy green material. "That's really cute. Did you get a top to go with it?"

"Well . . . yeah." Kayla lifted another hanger from the rod. "It's kind of froufrou for me."

"I like it." Sarah held the pastel green and pink plaid blouse up next to the skirt.

"You're not just saying that?"

"No, it'll look great on you. Wear it to church Sunday."

"Well . . . okay." Kayla hung the clothes back in the closet, and when she turned around, Sarah thought her face was a little flushed. "My mom says green goes with red hair."

"Well, sure. And your green eyes. That's a no-brainer. Green eyes are spectacular. I'm stuck with everyday blue eyes and dishwater blond hair."

Kayla smiled. "I like your hair. Come on. I'll ride back with you as far as the Romney Road."

"Sarah, you come again," Mrs. Bergeron said as they entered the kitchen.

"Thank you."

"Here, just a second." She put a dozen cookies in a plastic zipper bag. "Can you carry these?"

"Yes, ma'am. I've got a saddle bag for cookies and such." Sarah grinned, and Mrs. Bergeron smiled back. She wasn't as pretty as Sarah's own mother had been, but Sarah thought she was a nice, normal mom, and she envied Kayla in that moment. She wanted to tell Kayla somehow to appreciate her mom and dad, to be thankful for every day she had with them, but she didn't know how to say all of that without sounding weird.

Outside, Trudy and two of Kayla's brothers were patting the horses.

"You brats get away," Kayla growled.

"Aw, you're tough," said Teddy, the ten-year-old.

"Tougher than you." Kayla untied Cracker and jumped up on his back.

"'Bye, Sarah," Trudy called.

Sarah grinned and waved at her. "See you, Spinster."

They jogged along companionably with the horses side by side when the trail allowed it. Kayla chattered on about the horses and places they could ride. She even suggested a horseback camping trip.

"I don't know," said Sarah. "I'd have to ask Uncle Joe."

They separated at the Romney Road, and Sarah trotted Icicle the last two miles back to the ranch at an even gait. It was approaching noon, and Uncle Joe was in the barn polishing Jackson's saddle. Sarah brushed Icicle down and let him drink a bucket of water before she turned him loose.

"I'll go start lunch," she said, and Uncle Joe nodded without looking up.

When he came in and washed at the sink fifteen minutes later, Sarah had a steak frying and a passable salad and rolls from the store on the table.

"They're coming for Jackson tomorrow." Uncle Joe tossed his hat on the bookshelf beside the door and sat down at the table.

"You're done training him?"

"Yup. Last lesson this morning. That horse knows more than I do."

"I doubt it," Sarah said. "But he knows a lot more than he did when he came here, or you wouldn't have taken him on in the first place."

Uncle Joe said nothing to that, but he smiled a little. "You praying?"

They bowed their heads, and Sarah offered the blessing.

"Are we still going to Borden Corners this afternoon?" she asked, as he divided the steak between them.

"Sure. Did you tire your gray out this morning?"

"Not too bad, but I think I'll take Clover. We went over to Bergerons' this morning. Kayla's mother gave me some cookies." Sarah jerked her head toward the bag she had left on the counter.

He nodded. "You're determined to keep both horses in shape?"

"Yes, sir . . . I . . . I want to. If you don't mind."

He shrugged. "Up to you."

"You think I'm foolish?"

"A little overzealous maybe."

Sarah ate in silence.

IO

They rode mostly without speaking that afternoon, the long miles of sagebrush and juniper rolling away. Uncle Joe would occasionally point out a landmark, and Sarah tried to keep them straight. They had looked at the map the night before, and Uncle Joe had pointed out the trails he had already shown her and the route they would take to Borden Corners.

Clover kept up with Zorro by loping occasionally when her smooth trot failed to keep her close to the long-legged black. When they were within half a mile of the intersection that was their goal, Uncle Joe led Sarah off the trail to water the horses and rest at a small stream.

"So, what's at Borden Corners?" Sarah asked, watching the muscles on Clover's neck ripple as she swallowed the cold water greedily.

"Nothing much. It's where the highway crosses the Grindstone Road. Some old-timer named Borden used to live out there, is all."

"No town or gas station or anything?"

He shrugged. "Last time I checked, there was a juniper bush."

Sarah laughed. She was getting used to Uncle Joe's way of talking, or not talking.

"Did you and your mother pay a registration fee for this ride coming up?"

Sarah bit her upper lip and stroked Clover's neck. "Yes. It wasn't much though."

"Junior and Rose dropped by this morning while you were at Bergerons'."

Sarah looked at him then. He was sitting on a rock by the stream bank, his black Stetson shading his eyes, Zorro's reins trailing slack from his hand.

"We ate some of your doughnuts, since you and Kayla were too hepped up to eat them."

Sarah shrugged. "You paid for them."

"Junior says I ought to let you go to the ride."

Sarah's heart began to pound.

"I . . . I need a sponsor. Do you think Junior or Miss Rose would ride with me?"

"Nope."

"Oh." Her hopes were dashed, and she stroked Clover's flank, trying to hide her disappointment.

"Rose doesn't ride enough," Uncle Joe said. "She'd kill herself if she tried to go a hundred miles in one day. Anyway, I don't expect Junior's cow ponies could do that ride. They're tough horses, but there's not one of 'em has the stamina."

"Junior could ride Clover," Sarah said. "That's why I've kept working her, in case I could get someone to go with me." Uncle Joe's face was shadowed by his hat brim, and she couldn't read his expression. "I guess you knew that."

"I figured." He sighed. "Your friends—the Moseleys—they were going to this ride, weren't they?"

"Yes, sir."

"Eric's folks couldn't keep track of you and Eric both?"

CHAPTER TEN

Sarah shook her head. "Eric's dad doesn't ride. He helps at the checkpoints, but it's only Eric and Mrs. Moseley who actually compete. See, my mom got Eric's mom to ride with her—that was after my dad died—and then they let Eric and me train with them. We all went to a ten-mile ride together. That's how it started. Aunt Becky—that's Mrs. Moseley—she asked the association if Eric and I could both ride with her at the Bandicoot, but they said no. We each have to have our own sponsor, and we just didn't know anyone else who could do it. But—" Sarah stopped. She was talking too much. Uncle Joe liked his conversations in small bites, and he was disdainful of people who chattered on and on.

He inhaled, deep and slow, then stood up, pulling Zorro's head up. "Let's ride."

When they had mounted, he headed out without comment, and a few minutes later they came to Borden Corners.

"You're right," Sarah said, bringing Clover up next to Zorro and looking as far north as she could along Grindstone Road. There were no vehicles in sight in any direction. "There's nothing here."

"Well, I wouldn't say that." Uncle Joe brushed a fly from Zorro's neck. "This crossroads is kind of symbolic, don't you think?"

"How do you mean?"

He turned and looked her in the eye. "It's a place where we can head any direction. North, south, east, west. Or we can go off the road altogether and take our own trail."

"Yes, sir." Sarah squinted at him, trying to understand what he was getting at.

"I think today, we'll take our own trail."

"Suits me."

"All right then, what do I have to do to get them to change the registration from Laura's name to mine?"

Sarah couldn't speak. Her mouth was dry, and her pulse pounded in her throat.

"Is it too late to change things?"

"I . . . don't think so. You'd go with me?" She felt her throat constricting, and she looked away, off to the east, not wanting to cry in front of him.

"Well, you can't go alone, and it means a heap to you. I can see that." He bent over and scratched Zorro's left ear. "I'm not going to put that Junior Tate in charge of you. Now, don't misunderstand me, Junior's a friend of mine, but something like this . . . well, I'm not sure I want him to have that responsibility. Your friends can't help you, and I think you need your kin."

Sarah nodded and licked her lips. "Thank you," she whispered.

"Right. We'd best go home and do some calling, I'm thinking."

She turned in the saddle and peered hard at him. "You really want to do this?"

He shrugged. "Got nothing better to do that day."

Sarah smiled. It was enough, where Uncle Joe was concerned.

11

"You call Mrs. Moseley and give her the news, then let me talk to her," Uncle Joe said when their evening chores and supper were done.

Sarah's hand shook as she punched in the telephone number.

"Eric? It's Sarah. I—" She glanced toward Uncle Joe, but he was rinsing their dishes. "I need to talk to your mother."

Aunt Becky came on the line, her voice full of concern. "Sarah, what is it? Are you all right?"

"Yes, Aunt Becky, thank you. I just need to tell you and Eric, Uncle Joe says he'll take me to the Bandicoot."

"Sarah, that's fantastic! You mean he'll ride with you?"

"Yes, ma'am." Sarah felt her grin would split her cheeks.

She could hear Eric in the background, saying, "What? What? You mean she's *going*?"

"Hush, honey," Aunt Becky said. "Not you, Sarah. Eric's gone ballistic. Are you sure this will work?"

"Well, no, he wants to talk to you about it. We haven't worked out the details yet. He wants to know if they'll let him ride in Mom's place, since Mom—well, you know."

"All right, put him on the line," Aunt Becky said gently.

Sarah turned to her uncle. "She's ready to talk to you."

He wiped his hands on a dish towel and reached for the phone. Sarah went to the counter and wrapped up the leftover sandwich meat and put it away, listening to Uncle Joe's terse half of the conversation.

"Yes, ma'am. Well, you know. Sure. You think I can fix it if I call tomorrow?"

There was a pause, and Aunt Becky was evidently outlining a strategy for Uncle Joe.

"Sure thing. Well, the startup is at John Day, right? We're a whole lot closer than you are. Suppose you bring your son up here on the Friday? It's only about an hour from here to John Day."

Sarah turned and stared at him. She couldn't believe he was inviting the Moseleys to visit with them before the ride. If she'd thought about it, she would have guessed that was the last thing Uncle Joe would do. He wasn't much for socializing, Junior would probably say. After Uncle Joe's brief visit in California last year, Mom had told Aunt Becky her brother-in-law was reserved.

"You mean he's anti-social?" Aunt Becky had asked.

"No, more wary, I'd say," was Laura's verdict.

"His brother wasn't that way."

"No, Dan was more outgoing. Joe's just . . . well, he's alone a lot. He likes it that way, I guess."

Sarah had always liked Uncle Joe, but never felt she knew him very well. His visits were sporadic, and theirs to Elk Creek even rarer. Even now she didn't know him. Living in his house and getting used to his quirks and habits, Sarah met surprises every day.

"Well, we can manage," he was saying into the telephone. "Just pack up your gear and come. If you want to come Thursday, that would give the kids and the horses time to get used to being together again. Well, okay, whatever you think. I'll call the association first thing tomorrow."

He paused, and Sarah strained her ears, but couldn't pick up what Aunt Becky was saying.

"That'd be fine, ma'am. Well, I expect Sarah will fill me in."

He turned and held the receiver out to Sarah. "Eric wants to speak to you."

Sarah smiled and took the phone.

"Eric?"

"Sarah, this is fabulistic! Absolutely incredible!"

"I know! It's great." She looked around, but Uncle Joe was heading into the hallway, toward his bedroom. "Eric, are you coming here the day before, or what?"

"I think so. We're hoping Dad can come with us. Mom was writing stuff down. Can you send us directions to your place?"

"Sure."

"You have to get the horses shod within the next week," Eric said.

"Right. I'll ask Uncle Joe about getting a blacksmith to come. I have enough money to pay for it."

"And make them put leather pads on Clover."

"I'll remember," Sarah said. Her mother always had pads put on with the mare's shoes to protect her from stone bruises. "I can't believe you're coming!"

"I can't believe you're going!"

They both laughed.

"Have you met any kids there?" Eric asked.

"A few. There's a girl who lives a few miles away. Her name is Kayla, and she has an Appaloosa. We went riding this morning."

"Good. I'm glad there's somebody around there for you. Mom's telling me to tell you we love you, and we're praying hard for you."

"Thanks. I've been praying too, and I think God's been answering. I have a lot to thank Him for."

When they had signed off, Sarah finished cleaning up the counter and went to her bedroom. In one of the boxes in her closet, she found the thick envelope that held the information the American Endurance Ride Conference had sent her mother that spring. She pulled it out, and underneath it was her journal.

Sarah stared at it, then lifted it and held it, closed, in her left hand. It was her eighth journal, actually. Her mother had started them for her when she was a baby, and when Sarah learned to write, she had taken over keeping them. Whenever she filled one book, Mom would provide another. This one had a brown cover that looked like a paper bag. She sat on her bed, laying the AERC envelope on the blanket, and opened the journal to the last page she had written on. It was dated the day before her mother's accident.

> *We rode to Myers today. Mom has to go to town tomorrow to do research for the magazine, so Eric and I are going to ride to the lake and take our lunch. Icy and I have gone 80 miles this week.*

Sarah reached toward the bookcase for a pen and very slowly wrote the date on the next page. *My mom died July 31*, she wrote carefully, her hand trembling. *I am at Uncle Joe's now. We are going to the Bandicoot 100 together, and Eric and his parents are coming.*

She stared at what she had written. It seemed so bleak and uncaring. She wanted to write things the way her mother would have, pouring the words out, full of emotion, expressing on paper her bereavement, the disbelief, the numbness, the loneliness. And now, the joy she hadn't thought she could feel anymore. Was it only two weeks since her mother had died? How could she be happy again, so soon? The ride was so insignificant, compared to losing Mom! Sarah would gladly give up the ride and the horses, if only she could have her mother back. But still, her heart had leaped when Uncle Joe had said he would take her.

She got up and stumbled toward the bathroom, coming face to face with him in the hallway.

"You okay?" he asked, as Sarah came up short, trying not to look at him. She knew her eyes were red and puffy, and tears were running down her cheeks.

She pushed past him into the bathroom and grabbed a wad of toilet paper to blow her nose on. Uncle Joe wasn't into buying facial tissues. When she turned around, he was leaning on the door jamb, blocking her exit.

" 'Pears to me we need to talk," he said.

"Not your favorite pastime." Sarah immediately regretted she had said it.

"No, p'raps not," Uncle Joe admitted. "Come on." He walked out to the living area, and Sarah followed. He went for the roll of paper towels and set it down on the chest that served him as a coffee table, then sat on the sagging plaid couch. He patted the cushion beside him, and Sarah sat down on the edge of the seat, staring at the roll of towels.

He sighed heavily. "When I was your age, your daddy and I did everything together. Dan was a wonderful brother. He taught me a lot of things. We didn't always get along, but in a pinch I knew he would be there for me. You . . . well, you've got no brother or sister, and now you've got no folks. I guess I'm all you've got, so to speak. That ain't much."

Sarah sniffed. Uncle Joe didn't usually lapse into poor grammar, even though he spared words whenever possible, and she knew now that this was a sign of his discomfort in talking about serious things.

"Can you tell me about him?" she asked, her voice cracking a little.

"Who, Dan?"

She nodded.

He looked off at the washing machine that was squeezed into the corner of the kitchen by the back door.

"Well, I set a lot of store by Dan. He was my big brother, and, like I say, we did everything together. Rode horses and cut cattle, all that stuff. I got thrown once, when we were out riding a mile or so from home. I was shook up, and Dan took me home riding double with him, then went back and caught my horse and brought him home. I looked up to him."

"You loved him." It was important to her that he realize that and voice it, and he nodded.

"Yes. But then Dan got it into his head to go to college. I still had two years of high school left, and I was miserable. I was never so lonely in my life."

"Even now?" Sarah asked.

"No, I'm not lonely now."

Sarah wondered how that could be true, and if he were deceiving himself.

"But back then, well, I was used to having Dan around," Uncle Joe continued, "and when he left, it was awful. I'd never been alone like that. He was my best friend, you get what I'm saying?"

Sarah nodded.

"But I knew, when he went away, that things were never going to be the same again. Once he'd been to college, he'd want to do something else, and sure enough, when he came home that next summer, he was talking about being an engineer, and getting a job with some big company, and traveling."

"Those aren't bad things," Sarah ventured.

"No, I s'pose not. But they were different things, and I didn't want things to change. I wanted everything the same as it used to be, with my brother at home and riding with me. I was pretty selfish, I guess. And then Dan met your mother."

Uncle Joe was silent, thinking back over the years, and uneasiness crept into Sarah's mind. This was what she'd always wondered. Did the resentment linger in his heart?

"You didn't like Mom?" she asked softly.

"It wasn't a matter of liking or not liking. It was . . . losing my brother. I knew he would never live at home again, and I would never be the one he cared the most about again. Laura was . . . well, I could see why he was attracted to her."

84

"You could?"

"Well, sure. I'd have had to be blind to miss it, wouldn't I?"

Sarah smiled then and bit her upper lip to keep it from quivering. "Mom was pretty."

"Yes, but it was more than that. She was good too. Good inside. And she was good for Dan. She loved him, everyone could see that. I was glad, if he was going to get married, that he found someone like her."

Sarah smiled bigger. "I never knew if you approved of us."

He snorted. "Not up to me to approve other folks. But if it was, yes, I'd approve you. You are definitely a niece I would approve of." He ran his hand through his dark, wavy hair. "I need a haircut. Think you can do it?"

"Maybe." Sarah sat still. She didn't want him to change the subject.

He met her gaze and raised his eyebrows for a moment. "Well, when your daddy died, I was pretty broken up."

"You came for the funeral."

"Sure. But I didn't feel like I could help you or Laura. Your mom was strong, and I could see she'd make it all right. So I came back here, to my own place. But I was missing Dan something fierce. I'd missed him before, but I'd known he was there, in California. If I needed to see him, I could just get in my truck and drive a few hours, and there he'd be. But not anymore."

Sarah nodded. "I remember Daddy holding me on his lap in church. When he died, I used to cry every time we went to church because I knew he wouldn't be holding me anymore. Mom thought it was because it reminded me of the funeral. I finally told her."

"What did she do?"

"Held me. Not on her lap. I was too big by then. But sometimes, well . . ." She looked helplessly at him. "Sometimes, there's no substitute for a hug, I guess."

His lips curved in a bittersweet smile. "Long time since I had a hug. When I came down to get you at Moseleys' and I hugged you, I guess that's the first hug I've had in years. Well, the first human hug," he amended. "Horses don't count."

Sarah chuckled in spite of herself. She wouldn't in a million years have pictured Uncle Joe hugging a horse.

"Didn't you ever fall in love?" she asked, wondering if she was treading on dangerous ground.

Uncle Joe sniffed. "Had a girl once, back along. Molly was her name. I thought we might make a go of it, but . . ." He shook his head.

"What happened to her?" Sarah asked. She hoped Molly hadn't died too. That would be too tragic, and this family had had enough tragedy.

Uncle Joe shrugged. "She got famous."

"Famous?"

"Yup, kind of. She was a nurse. She had to be near the hospital for her work, but I hoped if we got married, she'd quit that and live out here with me. But then they asked her to speak at some school thing, to tell the kids about drugs or something, and everybody loved her. Pretty soon, schools and clubs all over the place wanted her to come and speak. Next thing I know, she's on TV talk shows, then she's writing a book." He shook his head. "Nobody with all that going on would want to live out here in the pucker brush."

"She broke up with you?" Sarah guessed.

"Not exactly. It just got so's every time I called, she was out of town, and when I wanted to see her, she couldn't arrange her schedule. So after a while of that, I just quit calling. 'T'wasn't worth it."

Sarah arched her eyebrows. "Maybe she misses you."

He shook his head. "Not hardly. Junior brought me a paper from John Day a couple years ago. Had her wedding announcement in it. She's Mrs. Doctor Somebody now."

"No kidding?"

"Nope."

It made Sarah sad, but somehow a little angry too. "She wasn't good enough for you, Uncle Joe."

He chuckled. "You the expert on love, are you?"

She looked down at the toes of her boots and shook her head.

"Now, your mother, she was a keeper, all right," he said. "Couldn't blame Dan. But seeing you two afterward, after he died, well, that was hard. It just made me think about Dan all the time. I stayed away for a long time after the funeral, longer than I should have."

"We liked it whenever you came to see us."

He nodded. "I liked it too. If I could have helped more, I guess I would have, but Laura, she was pretty independent. I didn't feel like she wanted me around."

"She always told me that you had your own life."

"Well, so I did, if you call this a life." He laughed. "Now, you are a fine young woman. If I'd come around more, I'd have known how big you were. I was a little surprised last week, when I first saw you." He put his hand out and patted Sarah's shoulder roughly. "I'm not sure I know what to do with you."

The tears were creeping back into Sarah's eyes. She swiped at them. "Sorry. I didn't mean to cry."

"Sarah, it's all right to cry. Sometimes it's necessary."

She tore off a paper towel and wiped away the tears that escaped her eyelashes. "I thought last night, when you were in the store—" She swallowed hard.

"What did you think?"

"I saw a lady that . . . that looked like Mom. A lot like Mom."

Uncle Joe nodded. "That's happened to me before. I'll see someone who looks like Dan from the back, or like my daddy. The day they brought that palomino, Jackson, I about lost it in front of the client. That horse is the spitting image of Dan's old horse, Dollar. Now, I know that horse has been dead twenty years, but it still gave me a turn. Just brought up the memories, you get what I'm saying?"

She nodded. "Tonight I was getting out the stuff about the ride for you, and I got looking at my journal. It made me think about Mom, and, well . . ."

"I get you." Uncle Joe held out his arms. "Come here."

She leaned toward him and hesitantly put her arms around him.

"Sarah, we're in this thing now. I'm not talking about the Bandicoot Ride. It's life. For the next few years, it's you and me." He squeezed her a little, then let her go. "If you want to talk about your mother, I guess I can stand it. And your daddy too. Or anybody else you want to talk about." He brushed at his eyes with the back of his hand.

They sat without speaking for a while, but Sarah felt it was a comfortable, friendly silence.

At last he said, "So let's look at that stuff. You got a map of the route?"

"Yes, it's in my room." Sarah got up and went for the envelope. She dumped it out on the chest in front of him, and they picked through the brochures and schedules.

"What's this?" he asked, holding up a white sheet of paper.

"That's a list of all the rides this year."

"Huh. Didn't realize there were so many."

"We were only going to two this year, because this was our first hundred-miler. We didn't want to overdo it."

"Dan was in that big one in California once, wasn't he?"

"Yes. The Tevis Cup. That's the big one. Every rider dreams of doing the Tevis. It's supposed to be the hardest, and it's definitely the most famous. They always hold it on the full moon in July."

"Good idea. Why didn't they hold this one on the full moon?"

"I don't know. Just had to schedule it when there weren't any others maybe."

He nodded. "I hadn't thought much about riding after dark."

"We'll start early in the morning," she said. "You have twenty-four hours to finish."

"What's the average time?"

Sarah consulted a brochure. "Looks like it's around fifteen hours for this one."

"So we could be done before dark, if all goes well."

"Right."

He smiled. "Well, that's not so bad."

"Last year's winner made it in eleven hours and four minutes," she said, consulting the paper.

"Not bad, not bad," Uncle Joe mused.

She held out a yellow diagram. "This shows the changes in elevation, and gives the distances between the vet checks. There's a rest stop about every twenty miles, plus one at the ninety-mile mark. It tells at the bottom what the terrain in each section is like."

He took it and scanned it. "Yes, we are going through some mountains, aren't we?"

"Sure are. Maybe we ought to do some steeper trails next week, for practice."

"I had no idea." He scrutinized the information below the elevation chart. "Dirt, woods, bridge, railroad underpass, stream, blacktop, woods, dirt, railroad track, brush, grass, stream, woods . . . elevation four thousand, one hundred feet. Man, this is a rugged course."

"Yes, sir." Sarah watched his face.

He looked up and smiled reassurance. "Not too rugged for us."

She grinned then. "It's going to be great!"

Uncle Joe nodded. "You bet it is."

12

They rode every day after that. Sarah alternated Icicle and Clover, putting the most miles on Icicle. Uncle Joe stuck mostly with Zorro, but he rode Clover twice and Ranger once.

"Poor old Ranger's being neglected," he explained.

"Are you going to ride Zorro in the Bandicoot?" Sarah asked on Saturday. "I thought you'd want to ride Clover."

"No offense to you or Laura's memory, but I think Zorro can handle it. If you want to ease up on Clover and just concentrate on the gray, it might pay off."

"All right," Sarah agreed. "I'd hate to let Clover get out of condition though. I'll keep taking her out for shorter rides mornings, but if she's not doing the hundred-miler, she sure doesn't need so much of my time."

When Jackson left, they drove a hundred miles and picked up a rangy roan mare, Celeste. Her owner wanted to ride her in barrel races, but Uncle Joe was doubtful. She was so tall, it was hard to make her turn tight around the barrels.

"Now, this mare could make a good trail horse," he said the second day.

Sarah leaned on the fence and observed Celeste's gait as he cantered her around the barrels.

"You should just tell the owner she's not suited for this," she called when Uncle Joe brought the mare to the fence.

"I tried, but the kid still wants to ride barrels, and this is the best horse he's got."

He worked Celeste, Buzz, and Rocky every day, and continued to polish Penny's gaits.

The blacksmith came on Monday while Uncle Joe was putting Buzz through his paces. He came out of the ring to discuss the farrier's work with him.

"Not on our usual schedule," Sam Lincoln said. "You've got a special job here?"

"Yes, my niece's horse needs shoes with caulks for an endurance ride."

"What, the Bandicoot?"

"Yes."

"You want pads?"

"I think so," Sarah said. She hadn't used pads on Icicle for the shorter rides, but she knew the ordeal she was about to put him through would be grueling.

"Better do Zorro too," Uncle Joe said.

"I just did him four weeks ago." Sam frowned, running a hand through his graying hair.

"I know, but I think I want the pads on him. He's never been a hundred miles in one day before. Rather play it safe."

"All right," said Lincoln.

"What about Clover?" Uncle Joe asked.

"I—well—" Sarah stammered.

"Better have her done, just in case," Uncle Joe decided. "If anything happens to Icicle or Zorro, she'll be ready."

Sarah nodded. "Thanks. I'm paying for it."

"In a pig's eye." Uncle Joe turned, stalked back to the training ring, and mounted the bay gelding.

"So you're kin to Joe?" Lincoln asked, rubbing his chin.

"I'm his niece, Sarah. I live here now."

"Huh. That must be quite an adjustment for Joe."

"Yes, sir."

"You don't look like him."

"Everyone tells me that."

"Sorry. Well, bring out the first horse."

Sarah led Clover out and hitched her, watching with fascination as the farrier rasped off the nail heads and pulled off the old shoes. They were quite worn, as Icicle and Clover had last been shod before the Dry Branch Ride in June.

"Do you do this often?" Lincoln asked, clipping down the thick horn on Clover's left front foot with a pair of nippers. "Ride competitively, I mean."

"This is the second time this year," Sarah said. "I've been doing two or three rides a year."

"I'll be at the Bandicoot. They have a farrier at some of the checkpoints. I'll expect to see you and Joe." He reached toward his tool box for a rasp. "Never knew Joe to do something like this."

"He never has before. And I've never done a ride this long."

"Well, I wish you luck. This little mare's good at it, I'll wager."

"Yes, sir, she was best conditioned at the Dry Branch Ride in June."

"That's not around here."

"No, sir, it's down in California. It's a fifty-miler."

"Hm. I do the fifty-miler in Boise every year."

By the time Uncle Joe brought Buzz in, Sarah and Sam Lincoln were friends, and Sam was shoeing Icicle. When he didn't have nails in his mouth, Sam told stories about difficult horses he had shod.

"Now, that Ranger of Joe's, he's gentle as a kitten," he said. "But Joe had a horse here a couple of years back that wouldn't let you pick up his back feet. What a time we had. Finally had to cast him to shoe him. Joe was so mad! Next time I came around, the horse was gone. He wouldn't put up with that."

"Couldn't he train him to behave?" Sarah was amazed.

"I dunno." Sam glanced up as Uncle Joe led the bay gelding in. "Say, Joe, what happened to that mean dun you had a while back?"

"Ha! You don't want to know." When Sam put Icicle's foot down, Uncle Joe unhooked one side of the cross ties and led Buzz past them. Sarah hooked the snap back on the gelding's halter.

"Yes, I do want to know," said Sam, moving his tool box around to the other side.

"I took him to the auction in Pendleton. That horse was ruined. He could have been a good little cow horse, but somebody let him get away with meanness."

"Couldn't you gentle him, Uncle Joe?" Sarah asked.

"Maybe, in about twenty years. Couldn't waste my time on him. I thought when I took him that I could fix his habits, but I found out he was worse than I knew. Waste of time and money. Oh, I could have put hundreds of hours into it and made an example of him, showing off the meanest horse in Oregon, turned gentle, just to puff up my pride, but it wasn't worth it." He hooked Buzz in the second set of cross ties and loosened the cinch.

"Most I've ever heard Joe talk," said Sam.

Word of the Pipers' plans for the competition spread. Kayla Bergeron came often to ride with Sarah, and Junior joined Uncle Joe and his niece once on a lengthy ramble into the foothills beyond his ranch.

On a fine morning Sarah and Kayla rode their horses across Junior's range land and ended up on the paved road a couple of miles from the Piper Ranch.

"Let's stop in and see Miss Rose," Kayla suggested.

"She's invited me," Sarah admitted. "Do you think it's okay to just drop in?"

"Sure."

Kayla and Cracker led the way up the dusty driveway leading to Rose Zucker's little clapboard ranch house. Despite the August heat, green plants bloomed in hanging baskets above the porch railings. Mrs. Zucker was standing in the middle of a corral that edged the driveway, and a dozen sheep and a few goats crowded around her as she distributed the contents of a bucket.

She grinned and waved to the girls, dumped out the rest of the treats from the bucket, and met them at the fence.

"Well, howdy! Glad to see you gals."

"Good morning, Miss Rose," Kayla replied.

"Kids!" Sarah stared past Miss Rose, at the little goats hopping among the bigger animals.

Miss Rose laughed. "Yes, those two are twins. They were born late in the season."

Sarah chuckled. "When Junior Tate said you had kids, I thought he meant you had some grownup children."

"And so I do. My son, Elliott, lives up in Seattle, and I have a daughter in Indiana. But these are my babies now."

"Do you spin wool?" Sarah asked, watching the plump sheep nudge and nip each other in their eagerness to get the corn Miss Rose had spread.

"No, mostly I just keep these critters for my paintings."

"Miss Rose is an artist," Kayla said.

Sarah stared at the woman with new interest. "Wow."

Rose nodded and smiled. "That's how I support myself out here. Don't have enough land to make a profit ranching. My husband proved that years ago. Since he died, I've concentrated on my art more, and I manage to pay the taxes and the grocery bill. Would you girls like some iced tea?"

"Thanks!" Kayla hopped down from the saddle and wrapped Cracker's reins around the top rail of the fence.

Sarah dismounted and pulled a lead line from her saddle bag.

"There, now," said Miss Rose with a nod. "There's a smart gal. Kayla, you should pay attention to Sarah. She knows better than to tie her horse up by the reins."

Sarah avoided Kayla's gaze. She didn't want her friend to think she was stuck-up or prideful. It was a simple rule her parents had taught her early. If a horse was startled and pulled back, he might break the reins, or the bit might hurt his mouth.

"Oh, Cracker will be all right." Kayla shrugged. "Sarah's just fussy, like Joe."

"Well, that's not a bad way to be when your animal's comfort is at stake," Miss Rose said. "Come along now."

Sarah quickly tied Icicle to a fence post far enough from Cracker that they couldn't bother each other and followed Kayla and Miss Rose into the house. While their hostess poured the cold drinks, she looked around the living area. It seemed that a picture hung on every square inch of available wall space.

"Are all of these your paintings?" she asked, when Miss Rose brought them their tea.

"Yes, I like to hang them for a while before I sell them. If I decide I don't like them, I don't offer them for sale."

"I'd be just the opposite," Kayla laughed. "I'd keep the ones I liked and sell the ones I didn't."

Sarah studied the paintings, most of which reflected the rugged terrain of Eastern Oregon. The sheep and goats appeared in several, and horses and cattle were also frequent subjects. She paused before a portrayal of a blacksmith at work.

"That's Sam Lincoln."

"Right you are." Miss Rose came to stand beside her, smiling. "I snapped some pictures one day last spring, when Sam was shoeing Junior Tate's cow ponies, and one of them was the inspiration for that painting.

Sarah nodded. "It's good. Has Mr. Lincoln seen it?"

"Not yet. I was going to send it to a show next month, over to Portland. But then I was thinking maybe I ought to give it to Sam. I need some money to pay my truck registration and insurance, but . . ."

"Maybe Sam would buy it," Kayla said.

Miss Rose shook her head. "That's the trouble. My paintings are getting pretty popular, and the prices have gone up. That's good for me, but it's getting so my friends can't afford them anymore." She smiled at them. "I'm sure I can get a good price for that. Maybe I'll paint another one for Sam."

13

By the following Sunday Sarah's excitement was running high. Becky Moseley had called to say that her husband was able to get Thursday off from work. The family would arrive late Thursday afternoon.

Kayla was jealous, Sarah could tell. After Sunday school, she walked with Sarah across the churchyard.

"I know Cracker could do it!" Kayla said, kicking a stone ahead of her.

"Could be," said Sarah. No sense mentioning the energy Cracker wasted in fretting, or the way he was winded after Kayla made him tear across the prairie at a flat gallop, her favorite gait.

"I sure wish I had somebody to sponsor me, the way you do."

Sarah could almost read Kayla's thoughts. She loved to race, and while she'd known the Bandicoot existed, the hundred-mile course was something she hadn't imagined a girl her age could conquer. Now the evidence before her of a fourteen-year-old girl preparing for the experience was driving her wild.

"Well, it's too late to sign up now," Sarah said. "Besides, you wouldn't have a sponsor."

"My dad could do it."

"He doesn't have time to train." Kayla's father drove to Romney every day to manage a hardware store. "Can you imagine him staying in the saddle for a hundred miles? He'd absolutely die."

Kayla sighed as they entered the church. "Next year," she said. "I'm going to do it next year."

"I hope you do." Sarah knew that if Kayla followed through and actually trained Cracker and was able to complete the race, she would be a better horsewoman. "After the Bandicoot's over, I'll help you work on it. It can be your goal for next summer."

The Carletons invited them for Sunday dinner, and Uncle Joe accepted to Sarah's surprise.

"Time you had a decent meal," he told her.

"We've been doing all right," Sarah protested.

"We've been doing fine, but this is good for you."

It *was* good for her, Sarah decided. There were napkins at each place setting folded into triangles and a butter knife that was passed around with the butter dish.

Junior and Rose were also included in the party, and Sarah decided they balanced each other well. Junior's brash teasing was offset by Miss Rose's calmer practicality.

Sarah sat beside Lissa Carleton, who would return to college the next week. Lissa looked especially nice to Sarah, wearing a floral print dress with a drop waist. Her hair was subdued in French braids, and her skin had a healthy, wholesome glow.

"Where's your college, Miss Lissa?" Sarah asked.

Lissa smiled at her. "You're so cute and polite. Just call me Lissa. It's back East. I'm going to be a teacher."

"Do you plan to teach around here?"

"Well, I don't know yet. I still have a year to go. I'll be applying for jobs in the spring. I'd *like* to come back to Oregon, but there aren't many jobs open around here."

"Guess we'll have to see what the Lord has for you," her father concluded.

"How come you went so far away for college?" Sarah asked. The East Coast might as well be on the other side of the world.

"It's a very good school, and they teach the Bible. My parents went there, and I wanted to, too."

Sarah turned to Uncle Joe. "Where did my dad go to college?"

Uncle Joe looked up from his meatloaf. "Uh, down in California. Cal State."

Sarah hadn't thought much about college, but a Bible college sounded nice. She had four years to find out if there was a closer one.

"And what do you want to do when you've grown up, Sarah?" Mrs. Carleton asked.

"I want to train horses."

She let the answer slip out, then glanced quickly at Uncle Joe. He was studiously buttering a roll, and she wondered if she had embarrassed him somehow. But her longing to train horses was not a sudden whim she'd had since her arrival in Elk Creek. She'd been thinking about it for a long time now, and wondering if she could realize that dream.

"Well, now," said Junior. "I guess you've come to the right place. Right, Joe?"

Uncle Joe looked over at his friend.

"Could be."

Junior came by that evening after church and sat on the front stoop with them, eating ice cream.

"I hope it cools off by Saturday," said Sarah. She and Uncle Joe had ridden thirty miles the day before on Icicle and Zorro, and had put twenty more miles on the horses that afternoon. The dry heat was relentless, and their mounts had arrived back at the barn both times dripping sweat with foam coating their sides under the saddle leathers.

"You two are gluttons for punishment," said Junior.

"And you're just a plain glutton."

"Hey, Uncle Joe, when you talk, you're funny," Sarah said.

Uncle Joe and Junior laughed.

Uncle Joe stretched and leaned back against the door of the house, looking up at the sky. It was not completely dark yet, but the first star was visible high over the barn.

"Guess I oughta build a deck, so we'd have a place to sit evenings."

"That would be nice," Sarah said. "But wait until fall, when it's cooler."

"I'll help you." Junior took a bite of ice cream. "Right after I fix the roof on Rose's henhouse."

Sarah wondered how much time Junior spent fixing things for Miss Rose. He had plenty of chores to do on his own ranch.

"Why don't you and Miss Rose just get married?" she asked. "Then you'd only have one ranch to keep up."

Uncle Joe snorted.

Junior stared at her, his spoon motionless in midair. "Who said anything about getting married?"

"I'm sorry," she said. "You looked so happy together this afternoon. I just thought—"

Junior took a bite and swallowed the ice cream. "Well, I'll take that under advisement, Miss Piper. But an old cowpoke like me and an acclaimed artist . . . Well!"

"Miss Rose isn't uppity," Sarah said.

"No, she's not," Junior agreed.

"Do you think she's smarter than you?"

Uncle Joe could no longer hide his laughter, but burst out in a choking chortle.

Junior scowled at him and sat up straight. "It's not a matter of one person being smarter than another. Rose Zucker and I are friends, and I'm sure things like IQ and education don't matter among true friends."

Sarah nodded, mulling that over. "You like her art, don't you?"

"Of course. I have several of her works hanging in my home. She is a fine painter, and I admire her and her talent."

"Not to mention her cooking," Uncle Joe muttered.

Junior impaled him with an injured glare.

"Besides, I'm not exactly illiterate," Junior said. "I read a lot."

"That's right," Uncle Joe put in. "He's got a complete set of Louis L'Amour, and I do believe I saw a volume of Agatha Christie lying on his kitchen table the other day."

Junior raised his chin. "I like to read the classics, not this modern trash."

"Oh, absolutely," said Uncle Joe.

"Louis *who*?" Sarah asked, squinting at her uncle.

Both men laughed.

"So do you two need a pit crew or something this weekend?" Junior asked.

"I thought you were staying here to feed my horses while we're gone," Uncle Joe said.

"Well, the way this girl tells it, you'll be back by suppertime. I thought you'd want someone to cool out the horses at the checkpoints while you drink lemonade, or whatever it is you do then."

Uncle Joe shrugged. "Guess we could use some support."

"You could drive our trailer around to the finish line after we unload," Sarah suggested.

"Sure, I'll do it."

"Well, thanks," Uncle Joe said.

"Kayla Bergeron is rarin' to go," Junior noted. "What do you think?"

"Did she put you up to this?" Uncle Joe asked.

"Not really. She mentioned it this morning, but I was already thinking about going myself."

"Maybe Miss Rose would like to go too," Sarah said.

Uncle Joe hooted. "Now we're talking a pit crew."

"Junior can drive your rig to the finish line," Sarah said, "and Mr. Moseley can drive his, then they can unhitch one trailer and drive together to the checkpoints."

"Might be good," Uncle Joe admitted. "We'd have an extra person to help with each horse when we come in to a checkpoint."

"Well," Junior said, cocking his head to one side, "Rose might not want to take a whole day to traipse around in the mountains."

"True. We won't know if we don't ask her." Uncle Joe stood up, reaching for Sarah's bowl. "More ice cream, kiddo?"

"Yes, thank you."

"Junior?"

"Don't mind if I do."

Uncle Joe went inside, and Sarah pulled her knees up, hugging them, looking up at the dozen stars she could make out now.

"That Joe's a character," Junior said.

"The first day I came, I thought I'd die of quiet," Sarah confided.

Junior smiled in the half light. "When he's got something to say, he talks, but you know Joe's not—"

"I know," Sarah interrupted. "He's not much for words."

Junior nodded.

"So how come everyone calls you Junior?" she asked.

He chuckled. "That's what folks called me when I was a little shaver, and it stuck. My pa was Myron, and I was Myron Junior."

Sarah pursed her lips as she considered that. She supposed Junior was better than Myron.

"So if you don't mind me asking, why *don't* you ask Miss Rose to marry you? Everyone can see you like her."

Junior was silent.

"Sorry," Sarah said after a minute.

"No, it's all right. You're pretty outspoken is all."

"So?"

"So, I'm not sure that's what either one of us would want. We both have our ranches, and we get along fine, but a person gets set in his ways, you know."

"I suppose."

He nodded. "I like my art in small doses, but you go over to Rose's, and it's all over the place. You can't rightly appreciate a fine painting when there's a hundred others elbowing it."

"I saw her house," Sarah admitted. It had seemed rather busy, but she'd liked it.

"Well, I'm more of the simplistic type. I admire Rose, I surely do, but that doesn't mean I want to live in the same house with her and her paint fumes and sheep."

Sarah smiled. She didn't imagine Miss Rose let the sheep in the house often.

"It's so sad about her husband dying."

"Well, yes, that was a difficult time for Rose. It was hard for all of us to accept when he died. But God knows best. Rose is . . . she's resilient. You know what that means?"

"I think so."

"She's tough. And now she's getting along all right. I think she enjoys her life the way it is. Before her husband died, they were trying to make the ranch profitable, and they were working night and day. She didn't have much time for painting. But look at her now. It's a whole different part of her life that she never really expected to happen. And she's relying on God more than she ever used to."

Sarah thought about that. Apparently Junior's faith went deeper than she had supposed, and she found she liked him more for knowing that. She decided to ride over to Miss Rose's again soon. Next week, maybe, when the excitement of the ride was over.

Uncle Joe came out, balancing the three bowls, and they sat quietly eating cherry vanilla ice cream and watching more and more stars pop out as the darkness grew.

14

On Tuesday night Peter Moseley called. Uncle Joe answered the phone and listened for a few minutes, expressing concern.

"What is it?" Sarah whispered, hovering anxiously at his elbow.

He put his hand over the receiver. "The boy's horse is lame."

"Hannibal? Oh, man!" Sarah pounded her fist on the table.

"Settle down," Uncle Joe said, trying to listen to Mr. Moseley. "Yes, sir, I hear you. Well, what did the vet say? Mm-hm. Mm-hm. Well, it sounds like you'd better scratch him, I agree. Well, no, don't do that. Will they let you change his horse at the last minute? Because they let us switch Sarah's sponsor last week, and I'm not riding the same horse they had down, either. No, sir, I'm riding my own horse. So if the officials will allow it, your son could ride Laura's Clover. I'm sure Sarah wouldn't mind."

Sarah tugged at his arm, nodding vigorously.

"Well, all right, you call them tomorrow and see if that's okay. And let me know how the horse is doing. All right. Thanks for calling." Uncle Joe hung up.

"Don't I get to talk to Eric?" Sarah cried.

"He's out in the barn with his horse."

"Oh. Well, what did Mr. Moseley say? What happened?"

"Eric and his mom had a long training ride Sunday, and Hannibal stumbled or something. Yesterday he was favoring his right forefoot. They iced it and hoped the swelling would go down, but it seemed worse today, so they called the vet. He thinks the tendon's strained and says the horse needs several weeks of rest. Can't do much about it."

"But they're still coming, and Eric will ride Clover?"

"If the race officials allow it. But this means we now have no backup horse. You've got to take extra good care of Icicle and make sure he doesn't overdo it this week."

"I will, I promise."

"Good, because I'm getting to the point where I'll be downright disappointed if we don't see this thing through."

Sarah could hardly contain her excitement on Thursday. She and Uncle Joe had thoroughly cleaned the little ranch house the day before. The Moseleys would stay at the one motel in Romney, but Sarah hoped they would spend a lot of time at the ranch.

For half the morning they worked to make sure the barn and the eight horses were spotless. It was very important to Sarah that they make a good impression, and it seemed important to Uncle Joe too. Sarah thought maybe he was afraid the Moseleys would think he wasn't taking good care of his niece.

Kayla and Cracker came before lunch, and Sarah took Icicle out to ride with them while Uncle Joe worked with his clients' horses. Celeste was showing improvement in her barrel racing technique, and she was quick to obey Uncle Joe's signals now. Sarah was beginning to think that horse might place in some local competitions, if the other horses entered weren't too good.

Uncle Joe had the Appaloosa mare, Penny, in the ring when the girls returned, lunging her at liberty, using only voice commands to control her.

Kayla leaned on the fence, her mouth open a little as she watched the mare walk sedately around the edge of the ring with no restraints.

"Trot," Uncle Joe said softly. The mare picked up her pace and trotted around the oval. Her snowy blanket and reddish spots were as beautiful as Cracker's markings. "Whoa," he said, low, from the center of the ring, and Penny stopped dead. Uncle Joe waited five seconds. "Walk on."

He went to stand by the gate, and when the mare reached him, he said, "Whoa," again. She stopped, and he snapped a lead line on her halter and stroked her neck.

"How did you ever get her to do that?" Kayla asked in amazement.

Uncle Joe smiled and brought Penny out of the ring, walking with her toward the barn.

"Sometimes I think he's deaf," Kayla said.

"He talks when he wants to," Sarah told her.

Kayla sighed and shook her head. "What time are we leaving Saturday morning?"

"Four o'clock. Don't be late."

"I won't. Junior and Miss Rose are picking me up. Are we riding tomorrow?"

"I think I'll take Eric out so he can get used to Clover. It will just be trotting, and you won't like it."

Kayla grimaced. "Cracker fidgets when you trot for miles."

"That's what you have to do for a long distance competition. You can't gallop a hundred miles. It takes patience."

"Well, maybe I'll come over. If not, I'll see you Saturday."

Kayla swung onto Cracker's back and galloped hard down the driveway.

Uncle Joe came out of the barn and looked after her, shaking his head. "That kid's going to ruin a good horse, if she doesn't break her neck first." He eyed Sarah testily. "You didn't race Icicle in this heat, did you?"

"No, sir. I told Kayla it was too hot, and Icy's too valuable."

"How far did you go?"

"Ten miles. Kayla and Cracker both hated it, because I wouldn't let Icy run."

He nodded.

"I thought I'd better give Clover a longer stretch this afternoon so she'll be ready for Eric, then ease off tomorrow."

"Twenty miles today, six or eight with Eric tomorrow," Uncle Joe agreed. He had been reading up on conditioning for endurance riding.

"Sounds about right," Sarah said.

"All right, let's eat, then we'll head out for our long ride."

They came back at five o'clock. Sarah had feared the Moseleys would arrive while they were gone. She had left a note on the front door, and another on the barn door, but the yard was empty when they returned.

They walked Clover and Zorro to cool them down and went about their chores.

"I'm leaving Ranger outside tonight, so Mrs. Moseley's horse can have a stall," Uncle Joe said.

"Won't Ranger be lonesome?" Sarah asked.

"Maybe. If he puts up a fuss, I guess I could leave Buzz out with him."

He sent Sarah to the house to start supper. She made spaghetti and salad, and set the table carefully. They'd made a shopping list together earlier in the week, and they had shopped in Romney for paper napkins and tissues, along with the groceries Sarah thought they would need to entertain their company respectably.

She heard the truck on the driveway as she stirred the spaghetti sauce, and realized she had been worrying about the Moseleys. When she ran outside and across the yard to the pickup, Aunt Becky was climbing out of the cab on her side, stretching, and Uncle Joe was greeting Mr. Moseley at the driver's door.

"Sarah!" Eric climbed down beside his mother and threw his arms around her. "It's so great to see you!"

Sarah was a little disconcerted, but she hugged back. "Where were you guys?"

Aunt Becky stepped forward and embraced her. "Oh, it's been a long day! We stopped for lunch in Bend, and I thought we were making good time, but then we had a flat on the trailer near Prineville."

"Talk about scary," Eric put in. "I thought the trailer was going to tip over!"

"You folks all right?" Uncle Joe asked.

"Yes, we're fine," Mr. Moseley assured him, "but it was a bit harrowing for about fifteen seconds. If I'd been going any faster— well, thank the Lord I wasn't."

"Some guy in a phone company truck stopped to help us, but he was afraid of Siska," Eric said.

"We unloaded him, and Eric held him while I got the spare tire out," his father said. "Not something I want to go through every day."

Aunt Becky nodded. "I'm just glad Peter was driving today, not me."

"I don't think I'm ready to let you and Eric drive this far with a trailer," Mr. Moseley said.

"Let's get your horse unloaded." Uncle Joe headed for the back of the trailer, and they all followed him.

When the ramp was down, Aunt Becky boarded the trailer and unhitched her gelding, Siska. He was half Morgan, half quarter horse, a compact, dark bay.

"Let me just walk him around a little and check him over," Uncle Joe recommended, and Aunt Becky willingly put the lead line in his hands.

"I walked him before we loaded up again after the flat tire." She kept pace with Uncle Joe and watched the horse's stride. "Sometimes they strain themselves trying to keep their footing when you swerve like that." She shook her head, frowning. "He seemed okay, but he didn't want to go back in the trailer."

"Can you blame him?" Eric asked. "It took us half an hour to load him again, and he's usually a good traveler!"

Uncle Joe bent to examine Siska's feet, then handed the line back to Aunt Becky. "Just walk him over to the gate, there, and back."

He stood beside her husband, watching as she led the horse straight away from them, turned at the corral gate and came back.

"What do you think?" Mr. Moseley asked.

"Well, he looks pretty good." Uncle Joe stepped over to Siska and ran his hand slowly down the gelding's forelegs. Sarah knew he was feeling for swelling or hot spots. "Let's walk him a little more, then put him in the stall so he can rest up. Tomorrow we'll have an easy little trail ride, just to keep the kinks out."

Aunt Becky nodded. "Thanks, Joe. I'm relieved to be here with someone who knows horses as well as you do."

"It's good of you to put the horse up for us," Mr. Moseley said.

Uncle Joe shrugged. "The Romney Motel's got no stable, and besides, I figure you folks are doing me and Sarah a big favor just by being here." He glanced at Sarah. "When's our chow ready?"

"I'd better go check the spaghetti," Sarah said. "Eric, come with me!"

They ran up to the house together, and Sarah was just in time to snatch the lid off the pan of boiling water, before it foamed all over the range top.

"What a neat little house," Eric said, looking around at the combined kitchen-living room.

"The key word being *little*," Sarah laughed.

He leaned against the counter. "I can't believe we're finally here."

"Who's taking care of Hannibal?"

"Mr. Johnson."

Sarah nodded. She knew the Moseleys' nearest neighbor.

Eric looked out the window toward the barn as Sarah took the salad from the refrigerator. "I thought you told me your uncle never talks."

"Did I say that?"

"Yes."

"Well, it was an exaggeration."

"Good, because he doesn't seem to have any trouble talking to Mom and Dad."

Sarah went and stood beside him at the window. Aunt Becky was leading Siska around the barnyard, and Uncle Joe and Eric's father were watching, but Uncle Joe kept glancing over at Mr. Moseley, and the two men were definitely talking.

Sarah chuckled. "Your mom looks like a kid from here." Aunt Becky was wearing jeans, sneakers, and her green T-shirt from the Dry Branch Ride. Her auburn hair hung down her back in a braid.

"Well, obviously she's not, or she wouldn't have a fourteen-year-old son, Einstein."

Sarah gasped. "I missed your birthday. Why didn't you tell me?"

Eric shrugged. "It was the day after the funeral."

"Oh, yeah."

"It's okay, Sarah. Being here is the best late birthday present I ever got."

Sarah swallowed hard. It was strange, how she could be so happy and so sad at the same time. She looked out the window again. Uncle Joe was leading Siska into the barn.

"Come on, let's put the food on the table," she said.

"I can't believe you made this entire meal. Is this how you earn your board?"

Sarah shrugged. "Uncle Joe's not much for cooking."

"Your mom was a good cook," Eric said. "I guess she taught you how."

"Some. It's not hard. But if you're a really good guest, you'll offer to help with the dishes after."

"Uh, I was hoping Mom would do that."

"Oh, come on. I've seen you load your dishwasher at home."

"Your uncle has a dishwasher?"

"No, but it's fun to do dishes together, and it will give us more of a chance to talk."

Eric took a deep breath. "All right, but Mom is going to be shocked."

When they fed the horses after supper, Uncle Joe put Siska's oats in a bucket and set it on the trailer ramp. Sarah knew, before her uncle led the bay out, that he was giving Siska the same treatment he'd given Buzz the week before.

Eric rhapsodized over the horses. The Appaloosa mare, Penny, especially caught his eye. A new leopard Appaloosa, Misty, had taken over Rocky's stall. Uncle Joe was giving her trail and equitation lessons.

"So, which horse is your uncle riding Saturday?" he asked Sarah eagerly.

"Zorro, over there. The black."

"Of course," said Eric. He went to the stall door and looked in. Zorro was munching his grain ration. "He's big."

"He's fast too."

"How much training has he had?"

"For the ride? Well, just the last three weeks really, but Uncle Joe rides him a lot anyway, and he was in great shape before that. We went thirty miles last Saturday, and it was hot, but he did fine."

Eric nodded and looked toward the barn door. "Well, look at that."

Siska was in the trailer, nibbling wisps of hay from a net at the front. Uncle Joe was leaning on the back of the trailer, and Mr. Moseley stood nearby, talking to him.

"You want some coffee?" Sarah heard Uncle Joe ask.

"Might be good before we head out for the motel," Mr. Moseley said.

Uncle Joe put Siska back in the barn, and they all walked up to the house, listening to Eric describe Hannibal's mishap on the previous Sunday. He helped Sarah prepare the coffee for the men and iced tea for his mother, Sarah, and himself. When they carried the drinks outside, they found his parents sitting on the front steps with Uncle Joe sprawled on the grass nearby.

"We're planning to build a deck out here this fall," Uncle Joe said. Sarah and Eric sat down on the dusty grass beside him.

"That would be nice," Aunt Becky said. "Especially when you have company over."

"We've got some friends lined up for a pit crew Saturday," Sarah said.

"That's terrific," Aunt Becky replied.

"They're going to drive our trailer to the finish for us, then come to the vet checks," Uncle Joe said.

"My friend Kayla is coming," Sarah told Eric eagerly, "and Uncle Joe's friend, Junior, and Miss Rose."

"Who's Miss Rose?" Eric asked.

"She's a neighbor and an artist, and she has sheep and goats, and—oh, you'll like her," Sarah said.

They sat on the steps for an hour, until the sun went down behind the rolling hills. Sarah was amazed at the things Uncle Joe talked about. The ranch, the horses, and his training methods. He had studied the endurance riding rules well, and had apparently memorized them. He explained to Aunt Becky and Eric the types of terrain they were likely to encounter.

"We've never done a ride in country as dry as this," Aunt Becky said apprehensively.

"Well, the first half is in national forest, and we'll cross plenty of streams according to that map they sent," said Uncle Joe.

"Yes, and they always have plenty of water at the checkpoints." Aunt Becky said.

"Do you think you should carry canteens?" her husband asked.

Uncle Joe considered. "It would add some weight. Maybe we'll take one."

"Are we going to stay together?" Eric asked.

Uncle Joe looked at Aunt Becky. "What did you all do before?"

"Well, we usually started out together, or one team right behind the other. Sometimes they have a mass start, but if they staggered the starts, Laura and Sarah started together, and Eric and I would be next in line."

"Two minutes between starts for this one," Uncle Joe said.

"That's the plan, beginning at six o'clock," she agreed.

"At the other rides, if we were all doing okay, we tried to stay together most of the way," Eric said. "But if one team had a horse that was lagging, we'd send the other team on ahead, so they'd place well."

"Mom and I left them behind last time, at the next-to-last checkpoint," Sarah recalled.

"Hannibal needed to rest an extra ten minutes," Eric explained. "We finished about half an hour behind them, but we finished."

"We'll try to stay together then, if we can," Uncle Joe said.

"I'll feel better, knowing that," Mr. Moseley told him.

Aunt Becky smiled. "Now don't you be biting your nails while you wait for us at the finish line."

"Would I do that?"

Sarah leaned back on the cool grass and closed her eyes. *Thank you, God,* she prayed silently. *Thanks for letting me have this day.* Though she never would have thought so until now, it occurred to her that this day—this moment, finding utter contentment amidst family and friends—was more important than the ride itself.

15

Eric and his mother came early the next morning for a training ride before the hottest part of the day. They were saddling up with Sarah and Uncle Joe after breakfast when Junior's truck pulled in, and Junior and Rose Zucker got out.

"Hey there, Joseph," Junior called from the barn doorway.

Zorro and Siska were in the two sets of cross ties, and Uncle Joe ducked under the lines to get to the barn door.

"Morning, Junior. What are you up to?"

"I persuaded Rose to ride into Romney with me for some supplies, and we thought we'd drop in and meet your company."

"Well, I guess you're allowed."

Aunt Becky had left off brushing Siska and stepped forward. Eric peeked out from Clover's stall, where Sarah had been laying out the mare's tack for him.

"Junior Tate and Rose Zucker, this is Becky Moseley, and that cowpoke in the stall over there is Eric," Uncle Joe said.

Miss Rose held her hand out to Aunt Becky. "I'm glad to meet you. Did you have a good trip?"

"Well, yes and no," she chuckled. "We got here in one piece, so we're thankful."

"We're on your pit crew for tomorrow," Junior said, including Rose with his glance.

"Glad to hear it," said Uncle Joe. "Peter Moseley will keep you company. He's having their trailer checked over this morning. Are you two gonna be able to put up with Kayla Bergeron?"

"We'll keep her in line," Junior said. "You need anything in town?"

"Yeah, bring me some pop to take in the cooler tomorrow." Uncle Joe took a ten-dollar bill from his wallet.

"Sarah," Miss Rose said softly, and Sarah stepped toward her.

"Yes, ma'am?"

"I brought you a little something. It's in the truck."

Sarah walked beside the older woman, wondering what the mysterious something was. Had Miss Rose brought cookies or snacks for the ride?

When they reached Junior's pickup, Rose opened the passenger door and reached inside, bringing out a flat parcel wrapped in brown paper.

"Junior told me about how you used to ride with your mother a lot, and I know you must be missing her this week."

Sarah nodded, blinking at the stinging in her eyes that always preceded tears.

"Well, I'm glad you've got your Uncle Joe. He's a good man." She held out the package. "I know this won't make up for the loss, but I thought maybe it would be a reminder to you of your mother's love."

Sarah's fingers trembled as she peeled off the wrapping paper. Inside was a small, framed painting of a mare nuzzling a fuzzy new foal. The mare looked a lot like Clover, and the pride in her wide brown eyes was unmistakable.

"Thank you!" Sarah didn't try to catch the tears that streamed down her cheeks. She held the frame close to her and leaned over to embrace Miss Rose with her free arm. "It's beautiful."

Rose squeezed her and rubbed her shoulders. "I'll be praying for you folks tomorrow. I hope you have a splendid day with your friends and your Uncle Joe."

"I'm sure I will. And, Miss Rose, I'm glad you and Junior are going."

When she pulled away, she noted that Junior was quietly watching. She smiled and turned the painting around so he could see it.

"Look! Miss Rose made it for me."

"She showed me." Junior smiled at Miss Rose.

Uncle Joe and the Moseleys had come outside the barn, and Sarah held up the painting.

"Oh, how lovely," Aunt Becky said.

Uncle Joe nodded and smiled at her.

"That's really nice," said Eric.

Sarah smiled through her tears. "Will you help me hang it up in my room later?"

"Sure."

"Well, we'd best hit the road," Junior said. Miss Rose climbed back into the dusty pickup beside him, and they drove off toward Romney.

When the four riders headed out for their training ride, they took the first trail Uncle Joe had shown Sarah, across the open sagebrush country, then down into the woods to the bridge. It was almost like old times for Sarah, riding with Eric and Aunt Becky, but a couple of things were out of kilter. Eric was riding the horse her mother should have mounted, and Uncle Joe was in the picture on the big black, riding ahead of them in silence. Sarah, Eric, and Aunt Becky talked about ordinary, mundane things, the kind of things that Uncle Joe usually didn't bother to talk about, and Sarah realized she'd missed the everyday chitchat.

When they came up out of the ravine near Junior's land, Sarah and Eric trotted on ahead, and Sarah pointed out Junior's herd of Angus, bunched up at the far end of his range.

"Where's his house?" Eric asked.

"It's beyond that rise." Sarah pointed to the southeast. "That fork in the trail up ahead goes to a spring."

"How far is it?"

"Half a mile maybe."

Eric looked toward his mother. "Can we zip down and see the spring?"

"Joe?" Becky asked, and Uncle Joe looked toward them.

"Sure. We'll water these critters."

"Come on!"

Sarah turned Icicle at the fork and cantered leisurely toward the spring. Eric and Clover followed. They dismounted when they reached the watering place, letting the horses drink deeply.

"This is a really neat place to live, Sarah," Eric said, watching his mother trot up on Siska. "You have all these great new trails to explore."

Sarah sat down on a flat rock, holding the reins loosely. "It is nice." She sighed. "I miss home a lot."

"Of course. You've had your whole world changed in the last month."

She nodded. "At first I was afraid I'd never see you and your folks again. And I didn't know if Uncle Joe really wanted me here."

"He's obviously proud of you," Eric said, and Sarah looked up at him in surprise. Uncle Joe and Zorro arrived, and Uncle Joe dismounted, so Sarah decided it was time to drop the subject. She and Eric pulled their horses away from the spring so Zorro and Siska could get at the water.

"Laura planned to visit you when we came to John Day for the ride," Aunt Becky said to Uncle Joe as they waited for their animals to finish drinking.

"Really?" Uncle Joe's eyebrows shot up. "I didn't know that."

Aunt Becky nodded. "She mentioned it to me when we signed up for the ride last spring. I think it's one reason she picked the Bandicoot, because it was fairly close to your place. She said she wanted Sarah to get to know you better."

Uncle Joe glanced toward Sarah, and the girl felt the irony of the close relationship she and her uncle had now.

"She hadn't told me yet," Uncle Joe said.

Aunt Becky smiled. "She was planning to ask you to come and see us finish. I don't know why she put off calling you."

"I would have gone," Uncle Joe said.

"You would?" Sarah asked.

He turned toward her. "Sure."

They rode home at a slow trot. The sun was high, and searing heat engulfed them.

"I hope it's cooler tomorrow," Sarah moaned.

Mr. Moseley was waiting for them in the stable yard, and Aunt Becky rode her bay over close to where he stood. She swung her leg over Siska's saddle and jumped down lightly into her husband's arms.

"Good ride?" he asked, giving her a little squeeze.

"It's beautiful out here. So different from back home."

"The trailer's all right, and I got the tire repaired."

Aunt Becky smiled. "That's terrific. Now all we need is good weather for the ride tomorrow."

They all watched Uncle Joe give the horses he was boarding their lessons that afternoon, and Sarah felt pride welling up in her chest. Penny especially impressed the audience. Sarah had seen her progress, and she explained to the Moseleys just how far the mare had come. She knew Uncle Joe would be done training Penny in a couple of weeks, and another horse would come to the ranch in her place. Sarah was getting used to seeing the clients' horses come and go.

After supper Siska was fed in the trailer again. Junior came by with the soft drinks and two boxes of ice cream. Uncle Joe dished it up, and Junior sat for a while with them in the kitchen, eating ice cream and hashing over the plans for the next day.

At eight o'clock Aunt Becky said, "It's been a wonderful day, Joe, but we'd better head for the hotel. We have to be up awfully early."

"I'd better get moving, too," Junior said. "We'll be here at four o'clock sharp."

"I'll just walk out with you and check on things at the barn," Uncle Joe said.

Sarah followed them out into the warm twilight and waved as the Moseleys drove away. Uncle Joe and Junior sauntered toward where Junior had parked his truck in the barnyard, and Sarah tagged along.

"Well, I'll see you in the a.m. G'night, kid," Junior called.

"Good night," said Sarah.

She and Uncle Joe went into the barn and looked in at each of the eight horses. Siska came to his stall door, a wisp of hay hanging from the corner of his mouth, and Sarah patted his nose and scratched under his forelock.

"Tomorrow's going to be great," she whispered. "You'll love it."

When they turned the lights off and stepped outside, Ranger whinnied and trotted up to the corral fence, stretching his neck far over the top rail toward Uncle Joe.

"You old flea bait," Uncle Joe muttered, ambling toward him. He scratched the pinto's ears. "You're all right, old fella."

"It's going to be fun tomorrow," Sarah said. "Well, hard work, but it will be worth it."

"Yup." Uncle Joe turned toward the house, and Sarah walked beside him. "Best hit the hay," he said.

In her room Sarah laid out her clean clothes and went to the window. The screen was in it, and a moth was buzzing at the mesh. She went back and flipped the light off, and the moth quieted. Sarah sat down beside the window, looking out at the barn. She could make out Ranger in the corral, his white patches gleaming. Closing her eyes, she leaned against the woodwork. It was strange to have her friends nearby again. It almost seemed like she and Uncle Joe were part of a very large family, not quite as chaotic as the Bergerons' household, but bigger and more solid somehow than any family she had ever known; a family that included the Moseleys and Junior and Kayla, and even Rose Zucker.

"Thank you, Lord," Sarah whispered. "Thank you for helping me not to be lonely."

She pulled the shade and turned on the light, then looked at the painting of the mare and foal. She and Eric had hung it on the wall at the end of her bed, so she could look at it when she first woke up in the morning. It did make her think of her mother, but her musings went beyond that. The vigilant mare would protect her foal. In her own mother's absence, Sarah had God to take care of her, and through God's doing, she had Uncle Joe.

She took her Bible from the shelf and turned to the spot in Isaiah where she'd left off last night. "And it shall come to pass, that before they call, I will answer; and while they are yet speaking, I will hear" (Isaiah 65:24).

"Thank you for answering my prayers, Father," she whispered. "You gave me everything I needed, even when I was too hurt to know what that was. Thank you for Aunt Becky and Eric and Mr. Moseley, and Junior and Miss Rose. But thanks especially for Uncle Joe. You knew we needed each other."

16

The sun was barely up when they unloaded the horses in a field of alfalfa stubble on the outskirts of John Day. Several of the competitors and spectators seemed to know Uncle Joe and stopped by to have a word with him. Sarah began to realize that her uncle was somewhat of a celebrity in equestrian circles.

Kayla was everywhere, eager to be part of the project, offering to hold horses and fetch things from one vehicle or another. Miss Rose helped Eric and Aunt Becky put on their numbered bibs. They had numbers seventeen and eighteen, and Sarah and Uncle Joe had nineteen and twenty, out of fifty-five entries. Junior checked the horses' feet and looked over all the straps on their gear. Mr. Moseley hovered close to his wife, seeming reluctant to let her and Eric out of his sight.

Each of the horses went to the team of veterinarians to have pulse, respiration rate, and temperature recorded. The statistics would be used for comparison at later stops.

"All right, Junior, why don't you folks head for the finish at Brogan and leave one of the trucks," Uncle Joe said when all the animals had officially passed the preliminary examination. "Our first checkpoint is twenty miles out at Crazy Spring. You can't get back there in time, but we should see you at Sheep Mountain."

"Right," said Junior, "then Murray Hill, Bonita Road, and back to Brogan."

Uncle Joe nodded. "There's a gate at the ninety-mile mark too. We have a half-hour hold at Crazy Spring and an hour at Sheep Mountain. We can eat lunch there with you."

"Got it."

"The first half of the ride will take us through national forest, and the last half's pretty much open country," Aunt Becky said. "I think the first half will be the hardest, but we'll have shade and water."

"You all take care," Junior said.

"Perhaps we could pray together before we leave you," Mr. Moseley suggested.

They all gathered around Uncle Joe, and everyone looked expectantly toward him.

Uncle Joe ducked his head and said, "Peter, will you?"

Sarah wished Uncle Joe could pray, but she knew there were just too many people. He had prayed out loud at the supper table for the first time only a week ago. She bowed her head and listened as Peter Moseley thanked God for allowing them to take part in the ride and requested His protection.

It was twenty minutes before six o'clock, the starting time for the first rider.

"We'll head out as soon as we see you start," said Junior. It was about eighty miles by road to Brogan, where they would leave one truck and horse trailer at the finish line and more than sixty by convoluted mountain roads back to the second stop at Sheep Mountain.

Eric peeled off his sweatshirt. "Could you put this in the truck for me, Miss Rose?" He handed it to her.

"It's warm now, but you may want that later," Aunt Becky said.

Eric frowned. "It's just extra weight."

"This trail goes higher in the mountains than any of the ones we've done before," his mother reminded him, and Eric reluctantly tied the sweatshirt to the cantle of his saddle.

Sarah, Uncle Joe, and Aunt Becky wore light, long-sleeved cotton shirts over T-shirts. Mr. Moseley brought them a bottle of sunscreen, and Eric rubbed some generously on his arms and face, then held the bottle out to Sarah.

"Better put some of this on. Remember how your nose peeled after the Dry Branch?"

Sarah laughed. That was partly what she missed with Uncle Joe—the memories. She and Eric had years of memories built up of the things they had done together. Well, she and Uncle Joe were building some memories today.

The first rider took his position, and they all watched the young man with the number one bib waiting on his horse at the starting line. The word came for him to go, and the horse set off at a trot, the ride officially opened. Sarah felt a thrill as she tightened Icicle's cinch. She knew the day would test her persistence, her fitness, and her horsemanship, but she felt there was a whole lot more to it than that.

Eric led Clover over close to her and Icicle. "This mare was always a good performer for your mother. I hope she'll do as well for me."

"She will." Sarah felt at that moment that she could promise anything on this golden day.

"Are you guys junior class?" A boy in a fancy red and blue western shirt, topped by bib number twenty-six, was looking them over.

"Yes," said Eric. "Are you?"

"This is the last time," he replied. "I'll be sixteen in two weeks."

"What's your name?" Sarah asked.

"Justin Earnshaw. My dad's sponsoring me."

"I'm Sarah, and this is Eric."

"You with your parents?"

"Eric's mom and my uncle."

"Those horses aren't purebred," Justin said, eyeing Icicle and Clover with scorn.

"Big deal," said Eric.

Justin held the reins of a flashy chestnut quarter horse. "I'll bet we pass you before Crazy Spring," he said disdainfully.

"Could be," said Sarah. "Come on, Eric."

They led the horses over to Uncle Joe and Aunt Becky.

"Here, kids." Aunt Becky handed them each a granola bar. Sarah stuck hers in her shirt pocket.

"I don't have a good place to carry it," Eric said. He had stripped the saddlebags off Clover's saddle to save weight, and his khaki T-shirt had no pockets.

"Stick it in your boot," Sarah said, smiling.

"Oh, right." Eric rolled his eyes.

"Here, give it to me," his mother said. She put it in the pocket of her green cotton shirt. "Eric, I'm afraid you're going to get sun-burned."

"I used the sunscreen."

Aunt Becky sighed. "Keep your hat on."

"We'd better get you two to the starting area," Mr. Moseley said. "Your numbers will be up soon." He bent to kiss Aunt Becky, then boosted her into the saddle.

"I'll see you later, Sarah," Kayla called. Her eyes were filled with longing.

Sarah grinned at her. "We'll expect you to have lunch wait-ing!"

"Just jog along slow, and we'll catch up to you," Uncle Joe reminded Eric.

"Got it," Eric said.

"Joe Piper!"

They all turned toward the voice. A man in faded jeans and a chambray shirt was walking toward them, leading a dappled gray Arabian mare.

"Well, Mr. Branson," Uncle Joe shook hands with the man and looked the Arabian over. "Are you riding today?"

"No, it's my son who's riding, but I came to lend moral support. How about you?"

"I'll be riding with my niece, Sarah, here."

"You don't say?" Mr. Branson nodded and smiled at Sarah. "I wish you the best. Joe, I've been meaning to call you. I've got a new mare I'd like you to take for a few weeks. She's as sweet as they come at home, but she comes all unstrung when I get her in the show ring."

Uncle Joe considered. "Is she entered in any more shows this season?"

"The one at the fairgrounds in Eugene next week, but I'm thinking I might have to scratch her."

"Well, maybe I'll ride over there and take a look, if you're going. If you decide not to take her to the show, just call me, and I'll see if I can make room for her right away."

"That would be great, Joe. Thanks! I'd like you to put her in shape for next season."

"Sure. We've got to mount up, but maybe I'll see you later. If not, call me."

"Dad, hurry up!" A tall young man called, and Branson waved at him. "Excuse me. Good to meet you, Sarah. Good luck!" He led the horse away.

Eric and his mother mounted and walked Clover and Siska into the starting area.

"Numbers seventeen and eighteen," the secretary announced, "Becky and Eric Moseley. Time out, 6:28."

"Go," said the starter, and they urged the horses forward. Eric looked back and threw Sarah a huge grin.

She swung into the saddle and eased Icicle into the starting area beside Uncle Joe and Zorro.

Eric and Aunt Becky trotted off across open ground, following the marked trail toward the boundary of the Strawberry Mountain Wilderness. They grew smaller and smaller, and Sarah felt her stomach flutter a little with nerves. Icicle was eager too and whinnied loudly for his stablemate.

"Numbers nineteen and twenty, Joe and Sarah Piper," said the secretary. "Time out, 6:30."

"Go," said the starter, and they trotted out together. A hundred yards out, Uncle Joe urged Zorro into his ground-eating canter, and Icicle followed suit. In less than five minutes, they had caught up with Eric and Aunt Becky.

"Can we canter for awhile?" Eric asked. His eyes were very bright.

"As long as we keep it easy, and don't let them overdo it first thing," Aunt Becky said. "We'll have some slow going later, so if we want to average seven or eight miles an hour, we ought to move while we can."

They rode in silence for a couple of miles, then crossed a paved road. Far ahead Sarah could see the forest. The horses sloshed through Little Pine Creek, then cantered on. The trail led for a ways along the outside of a cattle fence, then angled away from the road, toward the trees.

The path was still wide and well-traveled when they entered the shade of the ponderosa pines. Eric jogged along beside his mother, and Uncle Joe and Sarah came behind them. They began to climb gradually.

"This is the lower part of Canyon Mountain," Uncle Joe said. He had studied a contour map for days. "We're in the national forest now."

On and on they rode, higher and higher, but still in the shade of the stately pines. Then it was down and down, into a valley between two rounded peaks, then up again, higher this time. On the high slope the air was chilly, and Eric began to shiver, even though the early morning sun still reached them.

"I'm freezing!"

He turned in the saddle, working at the knots on the rawhide strips that held his sweatshirt to the saddle.

"Stop for a second," Uncle Joe said.

Eric halted Clover, and Uncle Joe edged Zorro up beside the mare and untied the knots.

"There you go."

Eric took the sweatshirt from him with a sheepish smile. "Thanks, Mr. Piper."

Uncle Joe nodded and let Zorro fall back as Eric pulled the sweatshirt on and set Clover to trotting again to catch up with Aunt Becky and Siska.

Sarah lost count of the streams they crossed. There were three bridges behind them, she knew, but the horses had waded several creeks as well. Icicle always stopped in the shallows and lowered his head for a drink.

At one point the path was so steep they all dismounted and walked beside the horses to spare them the effort of hauling their riders to the top, and twice the downslope was dangerously abrupt. Uncle Joe went down first, leading Zorro, but letting him pick his footing. Then came Sarah and Eric, and finally Aunt Becky.

The trail was clearly marked, but they had to pay close attention to the uneven ground and choose the best way for the horses in rough spots. When at last they came within sight of Crazy Spring, it was after nine o'clock.

"That is the longest twenty miles I ever rode," Aunt Becky declared.

"I think we're over the worst of it," Uncle Joe said. "We'll go through Logan Valley, then follow Summit Creek for a few miles. There shouldn't be anything as steep as what we just went through."

"You hope," Sarah said.

"I hope," Uncle Joe conceded with a grin.

They stripped the saddles off the horses and waited as the crew checked the animals' pulses and respirations.

"Half hour mandatory hold," the secretary of the checkpoint told them. "If recovery is satisfactory, you can head out again then."

It was very warm in the sheltered spot, and Sarah knew the fierce heat of midday was ahead. Eric took his sweatshirt off and secured it to his saddle again. "Guess I've still got some things to learn," he said to Sarah with a chagrined smile.

They splashed water on the horses' legs and let them drink from buckets, then flopped on the ground and ate their granola bars. Siska rolled, thrashing his feet in the air as he scratched his back. Sarah wished Junior were there with the truck and the lead ropes and could hold Icicle for her for a few minutes.

When they had been resting twenty minutes, the veterinarian came around to where they were waiting.

"Ready for a p/r check?" he asked.

"Guess so," said Uncle Joe.

The vet went efficiently from horse to horse, while the girl assisting him wrote down the statistics.

After counting Icicle's pulse, the vet said to Sarah, "All right. Looks like you're in good shape."

Siska's heart rate had not fallen as much as the others', but Aunt Becky explained that he had just rolled. When the vet had finished with the other horses, he checked Siska again.

"Okay, you can get ready."

They quickly saddled up and walked to the starting line. Newcomers were arriving, their horses sweaty and panting.

They lined up and left the checkpoint at the same time, but quickly fell into single file. The trail was rough, but not as steep as the first leg had been, and Sarah began to relax.

After two miles they began a gradual descent into Logan Valley and were able to trot most of the way. They crossed McCoy Creek on a bridge, then came into the open valley. After pausing at a smaller stream to water the horses, they cantered along for three miles, then slowed to climb again. They crossed a railroad track and rode within sound of Summit Creek for half an hour, climbing steadily.

As they rounded a curve, a woman wearing bib number seven came into view, leading a dun gelding.

"Got trouble?" Uncle Joe called to her.

"He seems to be favoring his left hind foot," she replied. "Thought I'd better walk awhile."

"Anything we can do?"

"I don't think so. I may have to pull out at the next stop."

Sarah realized they had gone nearly forty miles, and only two riders had passed them.

17

It was nearly noon when the Sheep Mountain checkpoint came into view. Eric pushed Clover up beside Icicle.

"I am *so* glad to see that banner," Sarah said. "I didn't want to complain, because I know we're not half done, but I am really glad we get an hour stop here!"

"Sore?" Eric asked.

"No, just tired. How about you?"

"I'm not used to this saddle, but I'm doing okay."

Junior, Rose, Mr. Moseley, and Kayla greeted them with happy shouts.

"You made pretty good time," Junior said.

"Did we?" Aunt Becky sounded fatigued beyond caring.

"Hop down, and we'll give you a hand," Miss Rose said.

The vet check was first, then cooling the horses down. Uncle Joe made Eric and Sarah sit down in the shade, but he and Aunt Becky helped the others take care of the mounts. Kayla was very helpful, eager to please. Miss Rose went to Uncle Joe's truck for the cooler.

Sarah lay back on the grass. "Wake me up when it's time to start again."

"Don't you want to eat?" Eric asked.

"Not if I have to move to do it."

When the horses were all on lines, munching hay from the back of the pickup, the adults joined them and laid out the lunch. Mr. Moseley offered the blessing.

"Quite a spread," said Uncle Joe. "We didn't pack those tarts or the pickles."

"Rose added a few touches," Junior said with a smile. "She thought you might be ready for a few surprises."

"This is delicious," said Aunt Becky, chomping a chicken salad sandwich. "I was famished."

Sarah had frozen two milk jugs full of lemonade, and the ice had not all melted yet. The chilled, tart liquid was more refreshing than anything else. She sat up and ate half a sandwich, a handful of potato chips, and one of Miss Rose's tarts, then flopped back on the grass again.

"What's next?" Aunt Becky pulled a damp, crumpled map from her jeans pocket and unfolded it. Even in the mountains it was hot, and she had shed her outer shirt and tied the number bib over her pale yellow T-shirt.

"Well, it will still be pretty hilly," Uncle Joe said. "We should be able to see Monument Rock from the trail, then we'll angle down toward Squaw Butte and Murray Hill."

"Hmm, looks like we'll follow this creek quite a ways." Aunt Becky traced the thin blue line on the map. Her husband leaned close to see where the route would take them.

"So, Joe, are you going to take this up as your regular weekend recreation?" Junior asked. He sat with his long legs folded, Indian style.

"This is too hard to be called recreation," Uncle Joe replied, sipping his lemonade.

"I'm just a wreck," Sarah groaned.

"You'd better catch a nap," said Miss Rose.

Sarah closed her eyes and thought she might be able to drowse off.

After a few minutes, Kayla called, "Hey! They've got ice cream cones over there!"

"Who wants ice cream?" Mr. Moseley asked. "I'm buying."

Sarah sat up. "Me! Thanks, Mr. Moseley."

They all licked their ice cream cones, and a companionable quiet settled over the group. Sarah saw that Mr. Moseley was watching Aunt Becky with a quiet, contented look. He seemed happy to stay on the sidelines and see her reveling in the hobby she loved. Sarah knew that Eric was supremely happy as well. There was no place else he would rather be than here with his parents, she was sure.

When Uncle Joe had finished his cone, he got up and made a round of their horses, checking their feet and clocking their respirations and pulses himself.

"How are we doing?" Aunt Becky asked when he sat down on the ground again.

"Pretty well, I think." He unbuttoned his chambray shirt. Sarah had shed hers, and sat in her pink T-shirt, sipping more lemonade.

"So, Junior," Kayla said wistfully, "do you think you'd want to try this sometime?"

"Me? I get enough exercise on my ranch."

Kayla's face fell.

"Best ask your daddy," Junior said.

"He won't. He said he's too busy."

"What about your mother?" Miss Rose asked.

"Oh, like she's not busy," Junior said with a laugh.

"She does like to ride," Kayla said with a spark of hope in her eyes.

They lounged for the rest of the allotted time. Sarah dozed in the shade for a few minutes, relaxing her tired muscles, and the rest of them chatted lazily.

The vet came to check on their horses.

"You have ten more minutes," he said. "All of these animals check out fine."

"Come on, Sarah," Aunt Becky said. "It's too early in the day for you to crash on us. We've got just under sixty miles left."

Sarah sat up stretching.

"You don't want to drop out, do you?" Eric asked anxiously.

"Are you kidding? Who said anything about dropping out?"

"Well, you complained so much, I thought maybe you'd had it."

"Sorry. I was really pooped when we came in, but I feel ready to ride again now. Are there any more cookies?"

She felt revived, and Eric seemed glad. She pulled her light shirt on again to protect her arms from the sun and branches. Aunt Becky brought the sunscreen from the truck, and Sarah and Eric obediently slathered it on again.

Junior distributed wrapped fruit bars, and Sarah pocketed one for herself and one for Eric, clapping her gray felt hat on her head. They saddled up and were ready when their hold expired, eager to press on to Murray Hill.

"One horse ahead of us was disqualified, and one had to wait an extra ten minutes," Sarah said to Eric as they jogged through a high mountain meadow.

"So how many are up front now?"

"Sixteen, I think. Two passed us, one dropped out, and we passed one."

"Wow, do you think we have a chance of moving up?"

"I don't know," she said. "It wasn't really our goal, but I guess anything's possible."

The scenery was breathtaking on that leg of the ride, with rock formations rising up unexpectedly, and mountains looming on either side. Through Monument Rock Wilderness and Whitman National Forest, they rode on and on. Uncle Joe set a quick, steady pace with Zorro, and Icicle had no trouble keeping up. He and Sarah topped a long ascent and looked back to find Clover and Siska had fallen behind them by a quarter of a mile.

"Let's wait for them," Sarah said, looking anxiously toward Uncle Joe.

"Sure. We might as well dismount and let these critters breathe while we wait."

Clover and Siska toiled slowly but steadily up the long hill.

Becky dismounted when they were two thirds of the way up, and Uncle Joe shouted, "You okay?"

"Yes, Siska just seemed a little winded," Aunt Becky called back.

Below them, Sarah could see two more horses gaining on them.

"Should we rest a while longer when they get up here?" she asked.

"What do you think?" Uncle Joe eyed her soberly. "Do you want to stay together or go on ahead?"

"I don't want to leave them behind," Sarah said with decision. "I think maybe the trip threw Siska off a little, but as long as he's in the race, I want to stay with them. Winning's not important. I don't want Eric and Aunt Becky straggling in alone at midnight, all tired and discouraged."

"All right. We'll stick together." Uncle Joe seemed satisfied. He scrambled down the trail and took Clover's reins from the boy slouched in the saddle. "Come on, Eric." He led the horse up the last ten yards to the crest, where Sarah waited. Aunt Becky plugged along behind him on foot, leading Siska up the last stretch.

"Get down and sit. Let your horse breathe," Uncle Joe said to Eric, passing Clover's reins to Sarah and reaching for Siska's bridle.

Aunt Becky sat down on a dry log beside the trail.

"The next stretch will be easier," Uncle Joe promised. "Do you think Siska's okay?"

"Yes, he just needed a breather, so I decided to walk him up the hill. He seems fine now, and I'm the one who's worn out."

"We can rest here a few minutes," Uncle Joe said.

"I don't want Justin and his father to pass us." Eric stood and walked a few steps back along the trail, staring down the long hill.

Sarah looked down the trail and recognized Justin Earnshaw on his chestnut. "Well, he didn't pass us before Crazy Spring like he said he would, did he?"

Eric smiled. "Nope."

"Did I miss something?" asked Aunt Becky.

"Oh, he's just a mouthy kid." Eric turned to Sarah. "Where's my fruit bar?"

"Here." She held his out to him, then opened her own. It was squishy and warm, sticking to the paper.

Justin and his father were halfway up the slope. Sarah glanced toward Uncle Joe and realized he was counting Siska's respirations. Her uncle looked up and winked at her, and she smiled.

"I think Siska's recovering," Uncle Joe said, directing his gaze at Becky. "Do you want to head out? We can take it slow on the next downgrade."

"Sure." Aunt Becky stood up and took Siska's reins, leading him to level ground.

Sarah led Icicle and Clover toward the low spot in the ridge, where she could see out over the next valley.

"Look, Eric. We'll be down there before you know it. Give me a boost."

He helped her onto Icicle's back, then swung up on Clover.

Uncle Joe said to Aunt Becky, "Do you want to lead and set the pace for us?"

"No, those long-legged animals would be running right over us. Eric and I are doing fine behind you."

"All right, but yell if anything goes wrong. Sarah and I had a powwow, and we want to stick with you two."

Aunt Becky smiled. "Thanks, Joe. Are we halfway?"

"Over halfway, I calculate. Maybe another five miles to the sixty-mile vet check."

"Only five more miles?" Eric laughed. "That's nothing."

Uncle Joe headed down the long slope, just as Justin Earnshaw's Quarter horse heaved himself to the crest of the hill.

When they were down the first, steep part, Aunt Becky trotted up close behind Sarah and called, "We can pick it up a little now if you want, Joe. Siska's got his second wind."

Uncle Joe didn't reply, but loosened Zorro's reins. The big gelding broke into a canter, and they pulled steadily away from the Earnshaws. Clover kept the pace doggedly, and Siska seemed to have taken heart. Uncle Joe looked back frequently, but the two smaller horses stayed close behind Zorro and Icicle, and the four entered the checkpoint at Murray Hill together.

Junior, Rose, Kayla, and Mr. Moseley each insisted on caring for one horse. Uncle Joe handed Zorro over to Junior and went over Siska himself while Mr. Moseley held the Morgan's reins. There was no mandatory wait, provided the horses' vital signs were within the acceptable range. All passed the veterinarian's check except Siska, whose pulse ran marginally high at eighty-six.

"Give him ten minutes," the vet recommended.

"Joe," Aunt Becky said earnestly, "You and Sarah should go on."

"No, we don't want to. Siska's not in trouble, he just needs a few extra minutes."

"I really think he'll be all right," she agreed. "His pulse is a little higher than average anyway."

"Yes, his beginning pulse was forty-two," Uncle Joe said. Zorro's had been thirty-six beats per minute, and Icicle's thirty-eight. "Let's just do what the doc said and let him rest a few minutes. He's doing fine."

At the end of ten minutes, Siska's pulse was down to sixty, and the vet let them go. Mr. Moseley helped his wife into the saddle and squeezed her hand. "We'll see you soon," he said. "If you need to take it slow, do it. Don't take any chances."

"That Justin and his dad are coming in," Eric said, as they trotted out of the starting area. "His horse is all foamy."

Sarah looked back, but she couldn't see them. "Kayla thinks you're cute," she said.

"Go on."

"No, really. Didn't you notice how she kept following you around and offering you soda?"

"Oh, please." Eric seemed more annoyed than flattered.

Within two miles they had emerged from the forest and descended gradually to open ground. Skirting buttes and ridges, they came to a vast, level area that supported nothing but sage and juniper.

Uncle Joe slowed Zorro, and the others gathered around him.

"How's Siska?"

"Good, I think."

"Can we make up some time here?"

"Let's try it." Aunt Becky looked tired, but determined.

"Eric?"

"I'm with you, Mr. Piper. Let's lose those Earnshaws."

Uncle Joe grinned and looked back behind them. Justin and his father were jogging down out of the foothills, and close behind them was a rider in a red shirt.

"Let's move," Uncle Joe said, and they rode four abreast across the prairie at a controlled canter, heading in a beeline for Bonita Road.

18

They rested the required hour at Bonita Road and gave the horses plenty of water and a small amount of hay. It was 4:25 p.m. when they clocked in, and Uncle Joe was in good spirits.

"Only twenty miles to go," he said jovially. "You up for it?"

"Twenty-point-four miles," Sarah corrected, "but, yeah, I'm ready." She sat on the tailgate of the pickup and pulled her boots off, rubbing her ankles. Aunt Becky sat in the grass, and Mr. Moseley was rubbing her shoulders and neck. Eric was letting Junior put a Band-Aid on his leg, where his boot top had chafed the skin.

"We'll stay mostly on the flat now," Uncle Joe said. "We'll be in the open again, but the worst of the heat is over. We'll pass close to Circle Butte and Juniper Mountain, then follow South Creek in to Brogan."

"You make it sound simple," said Aunt Becky.

"It is. We're nearly there."

"Even if we had to quit now, I feel like we've won," Aunt Becky said. "We've never come this far before, and I think we'll make it."

"You're doing great," Mr. Moseley assured her. "But then, I expected you would."

Eric lay down on the grass and plopped his Stetson over his face. "Wake me up when it's time."

His father smiled. "I've got to admit I'm surprised Eric's still in this. I really didn't think he had the stamina."

"He's plucky," Uncle Joe said.

"I'm doing okay," Eric insisted from beneath his hat. "I'm just resting."

"That's what we're here for," Aunt Becky said.

Junior, Kayla, and Rose again jumped into activity, watering the horses and pouring cool water on their legs. Kayla wielded the sweat scraper with vigor, then wiped each horse down.

"Hey, Sam Lincoln's here!" Sarah pointed toward the black-smith's truck across the clearing.

She and Uncle Joe sauntered over to talk to Sam.

"Well, you've come this far," the burly man said with approval. "I've been waiting to see if you'd get here. Want me to check and make sure all the shoes are on tight?"

"Sure," said Uncle Joe. "I'd say you did a first-rate job on those three horses we brought. Check the little bay too, would you? He belongs to a friend we're riding with."

Sam looked the four horses over and pronounced their hooves fit to continue.

"All right, there's a gate at the ninety-mile mark," Uncle Joe reminded the other riders. "It's in the valley between Juniper Mountain and Cottonwood. There's no hold, just a pulse and respiration check."

"You want us to meet you there?" Junior asked.

"The map doesn't show a road in there."

"There's got to be a road," said Junior. "They're going to have vets and a farrier there."

"Well, check with the race officials. If you can get in there, fine. We should make that gate in about an hour, if all goes well. An hour and a half at the most."

While Junior went to consult the officials, Kayla came and sat down by Sarah and Eric. "So are you going to school in Romney, or what?" Kayla asked.

"I don't know yet," Sarah said with a frown.

"School starts a week from Tuesday."

"Really?" Sarah wasn't prepared for that. Things were happening too fast.

Eric sat up and squinted at Kayla as he put his hat on.

"Do you go to school?" Kayla asked him.

"No, I've never darkened the door."

Kayla shook her head. "Wish my mom would let me stay home."

"Did you ask her?" Sarah couldn't picture Mrs. Bergeron teaching all the little red-headed youngsters, any more than she could envision her taking the time to train a horse for endurance riding. But then, mothers seemed to have hidden reserves of energy she didn't understand.

Kayla shrugged. "I mentioned it, and she just laughed."

"She's probably relieved when you head out the door for school in the morning," Eric said with a grin.

At five o'clock, Uncle Joe judged that Siska was doing fine and would be allowed to leave after the required hour. Junior, Rose, Kayla, and Mr. Moseley packed up and headed for the fifth gate.

"You got enough energy to finish this thing?" Sarah asked Eric as she pulled her boots back on.

"You bet I do. You're the one who was moaning and groaning earlier."

"I'm fine now." She felt more alert and determined than she had at the lunch stop. "Must be the adrenaline."

Eric nodded. "That and just knowing we're almost finished."

"So, still chugging along on your mongrel nags?" asked a smug voice.

Sarah and Eric looked up. Justin Earnshaw stood six feet away, with a sardonic smile skewing his features.

"I haven't seen you go flying past us yet," said Eric.

Sarah elbowed him, not wanting to start anything.

"I'm biding my time," Justin sneered. "You'll be eating my dust before you know it." He turned and walked away.

"He and his dad checked in a minute behind us," Sarah whispered.

"I know. So we've got to be ready at 5:25."

"If they pass us, it's no big deal," Sarah said.

"It's a big deal to me. He's so arrogant!"

"Don't hold a grudge," Sarah advised. "He hasn't really done anything, just made fun of us, and we're proving him wrong by staying ahead of him. That's what's getting his goat."

"Come here, kids," Aunt Becky called. They went over to where she and Uncle Joe were holding their horses. "Let's make our goals clear here," she said when Sarah and Eric had taken Icicle and Clover's reins.

"Our first goal for the day is to go home with everybody safe and healthy," Uncle Joe said, holding their gaze with his deep brown eyes.

"Of course," said Sarah.

"And the horses too," said Eric.

"Right. That's goal number two. People come first, then horses." Uncle Joe took his hat off, wiped his forehead, and put the hat back on. "Our third goal is to finish the ride, if we can do that and still uphold the first two goals."

"Is there any doubt?" Sarah asked.

"Not at this point, but when you get this close, it might be easy to lose sight of goal one or two, when you think you're going to miss out on goal three. Becky's right. Even if we didn't go one step farther, we've had a great day today, agreed?"

"Yes," Sarah said.

Eric nodded slowly.

"And the fourth goal," said Aunt Becky, "is to finish together, if we can. But if we're close to the finish and Siska's gasping, Joe, I want you and Sarah to go ahead, and Eric and I will come in at Siska's pace."

"No, the fourth goal is to finish ahead of the Earnshaws," Eric said, a bit petulantly.

His mother stared at him in surprise. "Is that kid really getting to you?"

"He comes and sneers at us at every checkpoint," Eric said.

"But you're still ahead of him," Uncle Joe pointed out.

"That's what I told him," said Sarah.

Aunt Becky held out her hands toward Eric. "You can't let this boy upset you. This is exactly what Joe was talking about. You're letting beating Justin become more important than having a good day together."

Eric looked down at the ground and kicked at a clump of sagebrush. After a moment, he said, "I'm sorry."

"Let's pray for Justin right now," Aunt Becky suggested. She looked around at all of them. Uncle Joe and Sarah nodded. Eric frowned, but he bowed his head.

"Dear Lord, thank You for bringing us here safely," Aunt Becky said quietly. "If it's Your will, may we finish this ride in safety. And please, Lord, let us show a good attitude to Justin. If possible, give us an opportunity to be a witness for You today. Amen."

Sarah felt a lump in her throat. She said, "I wasn't thinking about us being a testimony today. I was only thinking about the fun we would have. But you're right. We ought to show Justin some sportsmanship, at least."

"A Christlike attitude," Aunt Becky said, looking keenly at Eric.

"I'm sorry, Mom." Eric's voice cracked.

"Okay. Let's move on then."

Uncle Joe nodded. "It's almost time for us to start."

"Do we have a strategy?" Eric asked.

Uncle Joe said, "I think, if the terrain is good, we can canter for the next two or three miles, then slow down to a trot. A mile out from the fifth gate, we'll check Siska. If his p/r is high, we'll walk in from there, so we don't have a hold at the gate. If everyone's okay, we can move right out after the vet check. Then we repeat that pattern for the last leg." He consulted his watch. "We've got fifteen minutes. Looks like the vet's coming to check up on us."

Siska passed muster, and they were saddled and ready on the dot of 5:24.

"Good luck," the secretary told them as they awaited the word to start again. "You've got fourteen riders ahead of you."

"Only fourteen?" Eric asked.

"One was disqualified here a few minutes ago, and another is holding for some extra time. That one's questionable," the girl said as she made a notation on her clipboard. "You guys are in the running for the top ten. Go for it."

"Don't forget," Aunt Becky admonished Sarah and Eric as they set out, "finishing in the top ten is way down our list."

"Right," Eric said.

Justin Earnshaw and his father moved into the starting area as they left it.

"Let's move, Uncle Joe," Eric cried.

Uncle Joe laughed and urged Zorro into a lope.

19

The first few miles were easy, and Sarah reveled in the breeze they created, staying ahead of the dust their horses kicked up. She was tired, but it felt good. She and Icicle were old partners, understanding each other without any effort. And she was beginning to feel that way about Uncle Joe. That felt good too.

Eric looked over his shoulder occasionally and kept Sarah posted on the progress of the Earnshaws.

"I think we're keeping our lead," he said with satisfaction when Uncle Joe signaled Zorro to gear down to his smooth extended trot.

"How's Siska?" he called to Aunt Becky.

"Good, I think. He's not heaving. He could use a drink maybe."

"There's a stream up ahead someplace. We'll take a couple of minutes there." Uncle Joe held Zorro back until he swung into step beside Siska, slowing imperceptibly to match the bay's stride. "He's sweaty, but he's breathing fine."

Aunt Becky nodded and smiled at him. Sarah and Eric moved out ahead of them.

"Don't get too far out in front," Uncle Joe called, and Sarah waved at him.

"I like your Uncle Joe," Eric said.

"Me too. I feel a lot different about him now than I did when I first came to stay with him." Far ahead, Sarah could see a tree line. "That must be where the stream is."

"It's not too far."

"Distances are deceptive out here," Sarah said. "Could be two or three miles."

Slowly the trees grew closer. Icicle and Clover jogged along together, as they had so many times before.

Sarah turned and glanced back at the adults.

"Oh-oh."

"What?"

"Looks like Justin and his dad are moving up."

Eric looked back and consternation crossed his face. "I'm not going to be mad," he said quietly. "We've stayed ahead of them for eighty-some-odd miles. That's pretty good, don't you think?"

Uncle Joe saw the two teenagers studying their back trail. He looked over his shoulder, then said something to Aunt Becky, and they pushed their horses into a canter.

"Come on, kids," Uncle Joe cried, breezing past them on Zorro.

Eric whooped. "Your uncle's the greatest!" He flattened himself on Clover's neck. Sarah didn't have to urge her horse. When Zorro took the lead, Icicle leaped forward, and Sarah found herself gently holding him back from a dead run.

"We're lengthening our lead," Eric called, as they approached the tree line.

"Well, good, but we've got to slow down," Uncle Joe replied, pulling Zorro in. "Looks like quite a drop to the stream here. Take it easy going down."

He let Zorro trot up to the verge of the descent, then slowed to a walk.

"Do we need to lead them down?" Aunt Becky asked.

"I don't think so. Just lean back and go slow." Uncle Joe let Zorro pick his way down the stony path. Tall cottonwoods grew in the bottom of the draw, their tops rising above the sides of the little canyon.

"Watch it here," Uncle Joe advised over his shoulder, at a tricky bend in the narrow trail.

"Slow and easy," Sarah agreed. She leaned back against the cantle of the saddle. Icicle was feeling carefully for his footing with his front hooves.

Uncle Joe reached the bottom, and he waded Zorro out into the stream. It was little more than a brook, with a sandy bottom. Zorro plunged his nose into the water and began to drink. Uncle Joe eased the horse around so he could watch the others make the final few yards of the descent.

Sarah and Icicle reached the foot of the path and sloshed into the water. Sarah thought about swinging down and getting wet all over, but decided against it. Uncle Joe was watching Eric near the bottom of the trail and Aunt Becky a few yards above guiding Siska gently down the steep path.

There was a shout from above, and they all looked up. Justin Earnshaw and his chestnut were silhouetted against the sky above. Sarah gasped as Justin drove the horse forward, plunging pell-mell down the trail.

Sarah's eyes never left Justin, but she felt Uncle Joe stiffen. She started to yell, but the cry died in her throat as Aunt Becky squeezed Siska, snorting, off the path and Justin's mount crashed past her and slammed into Clover's hindquarters.

Clover stumbled, and Eric fell off with a muffled shout. Sarah saw, before her friend hit the ground, that Justin's chestnut couldn't regain his balance. Clover squealed and dodged, carefully sidestepping Eric, but Justin and his horse landed in a heap at the edge of the stream. The gelding snorted and thrashed, then got his feet under him and stood, shaking water from his muzzle, but Justin lay still on the bank, one hand trailing in the water.

Zorro leaped toward him, and Uncle Joe hit the ground next to the boy before Sarah could even breathe.

"Can you hear me, kid?" Uncle Joe's voice was loud in the draw.

Justin opened his eyes and began to scream. "Daddy! Daddy!"

"Justin!" The shout came from above, and Sarah could see the boy's father, on a magnificent palomino, peering down at them.

"Better dismount and come down slow," Uncle Joe called up to him. Mr. Earnshaw hesitated only an instant, then swung off the palomino and advanced cautiously.

"Eric, you okay?" Uncle Joe yelled.

Aunt Becky had left Siska with his reins hanging straight down, ground tied, and was making her way cautiously down to Eric, who was sitting up beside the trail, holding his wrist.

"My arm hurts," Eric said, his voice a bit shaky.

"Daddy! Daddy! Oh, it hurts!" Justin shrieked.

"Hush, now," Uncle Joe said, kneeling beside Justin on the stream bank. "We're gonna help you. Don't yell like that, or you'll get the horses all upset."

"Bullet!" Justin cried. He wriggled, straining to see his horse, then lay back moaning.

"Your leg looks bad. Just lie still." Uncle Joe turned to Sarah. "Check the boy's horse."

Sarah rode to the stream bank, jumped down, dropping Icicle's reins, and went slowly toward Bullet. The chestnut skittered away, along the edge of the stream toward a willow tree that overhung the water.

"Easy now," Sarah whispered, just loud enough to be heard over the rippling water. "You're all right now." She thought the chestnut limped on his left foreleg.

Mr. Earnshaw had reached Uncle Joe and Justin, and Sarah heard him talking anxiously with Uncle Joe. Justin still cried, his voice rising in a scream every few seconds.

When Bullet lowered his head and began to slurp water, Sarah eased up next to him, wading to her ankles, and made a dive for the trailing reins. Bullet jerked his head up, but Sarah held on.

"Settle down now." She patted the chestnut's neck and shoulder. "It's okay, fella. It's okay."

Bullet shook his head, splashing cool drops of water all over Sarah. She stood still, speaking softly, and the chestnut eyed her and snorted, then lowered his head and resumed drinking. Sarah looked back toward the cluster of people, where Justin had fallen.

Mr. Earnshaw was on his knees beside his son.

"Dad, it hurts awful," Justin sobbed.

"I know, Son, but we'll take care of it."

Sarah led Bullet over close to Icicle and lifted Bullet's left front foot. The edge of the horn was ragged, and the shoe was gone.

"Does this horse ground tie?" she called.

Mr. Earnshaw looked over his shoulder at her. "Bring him over here by my mare, and he'll be fine."

When she was shed of the chestnut horse, Sarah approached the group huddled around Justin.

"You okay?" she asked Eric.

"I think so. My wrist hurts, and my hip is sore, where I landed."

"How about Clover?"

"She seems all right."

Sarah nodded.

"Should we straighten that leg?" Mr. Earnshaw asked, his face ashen.

"No," Aunt Becky said. "Don't move him."

"Mr. Earnshaw, I think we'd better ride on to the next gate and send a doctor back here for you," Uncle Joe said, putting his hand on the man's shoulder.

"Will there be a doctor there?"

"Paramedics anyway," Aunt Becky assured him. "I don't think it's more than two miles to the fifth gate. We can be there in fifteen minutes."

"I—please, someone stay with us," Mr. Earnshaw said bleakly. "I don't know if I can handle this and two horses by myself."

Aunt Becky looked at Uncle Joe. "You and Sarah stay."

"No, Zorro's faster. I'll ride ahead. He can make it in no time. You and the kids wait here."

"But if you leave Sarah behind, she won't be able to finish the ride. They'll disqualify her."

"All right, Sarah and I will both go. That gray can keep up with Zorro." Uncle Joe looked hard at Eric. "Are you sure you can ride?" "Yes, Uncle Joe. My wrist hurts a little, but it's my right hand. If Mom helps me mount, I'll be able to ride just fine."

Uncle Joe nodded grimly. "All right, Sarah, let's go. Eric and his mother will stay here. And Becky, any rider that comes along, you ask them if they have medical training. It shouldn't be more than half an hour before some help gets here, twenty minutes if I can help it."

Aunt Becky nodded, her eyes large and solemn.

Uncle Joe reached out and touched Eric's shoulder. "You'll be all right, son."

Eric smiled. "I know. Just tell my dad I'm not hurt bad."

Sarah brought Zorro and Icicle over to the level ground, and she and Uncle Joe mounted. Zorro splashed across the stream, and Icicle followed. When they reached the far bank, Sarah looked up at the steep trail leading to the level of the prairie above.

"Do we lead them?"

"I think they can do it."

Uncle Joe lay down on Zorro's neck so he wouldn't overbalance him, and the black lunged forward, leaping with huge strides up the slope. Sarah leaned forward and hugged Icicle's neck.

"Go, boy!" The gray plunged upward, following Zorro without hesitation. When the horse heaved himself over the top, Sarah looked back for a second. Justin was a tiny form, splayed at the edge of the water, his father crouched beside him. Aunt Becky and Eric were near the horses. Straight across, at the top of the trail they had come down earlier, two more horses came into view. The riders halted, looking down, and Sarah could see Aunt Becky waving and heard a muffled shout, but couldn't catch her words.

She turned eastward. Uncle Joe and Zorro were already a hundred yards away, galloping toward the gate at the ninety-mile mark. She squeezed Icicle's sides and leaned forward again. The gelding leaped after the black, his hooves drumming the dry, dusty ground. Sarah realized she had never known before exactly how fast her horse could run. The wind caught her breath, and she couldn't help thinking of Kayla, and how she'd love to see this race.

20

They came to the gate before Sarah expected it. After streaking along for four minutes, they suddenly rounded a clump of trees and were in the rest area. Uncle Joe pulled Zorro up so fast that Icicle nearly collided with him, and Sarah flew forward, catching herself on the gray's neck.

Pickups, horse trailers, and an ambulance filled the tiny parking area. Two paramedics lounged near the ride secretary who sat in a folding lawn chair, his clipboard on his knee. A bibbed rider was holding the reins of a brown mare while the vet took its pulse. And sitting on the tailgate of Uncle Joe's black pickup was Kayla Bergeron with Junior and Miss Rose leaning against the side of the truck, drinking root beer and chatting with Peter Moseley.

The secretary and paramedics stood up when Zorro and Icicle thundered into the checkpoint.

"What's up?" the secretary asked. Riders didn't come charging in to vet checks.

"A boy's broken his leg back at the stream," Uncle Joe said.

The paramedics, a gray-haired man and a blonde woman, stepped forward.

"You're sure it's broken?" the man asked.

"No doubt. Could be other injuries, but the leg is bad."

"Compound fracture?"

Sarah didn't know what that meant, but Uncle Joe said, "Yes, sir. He's bleeding some. I put a bandanna around it, but not tight. You got a doctor here?"

"No, but we'll call for the one in Brogan to come up here and meet us. Can we get the ambulance to him?"

"I think you can drive to the top of the stream bank, maybe a couple of hundred yards from where he is, but you'll have to lug him up out of the ravine," Uncle Joe said. "It's steep. It's about a mile and a half back, I think."

"I know where it is," said the secretary. "I ride these trails all the time. I'll go with these two and let my wife take your statistics." He handed his clipboard to a woman who had come to stand beside him. "You hold the fort here, honey."

"Sure."

"We'll call ahead to the hospital at Baker," the female paramedic said as she and her partner headed for the ambulance, the ride secretary hard on their heels.

"Check the other boy too, Eric Moseley," Uncle Joe called after them. "He hurt his wrist."

Their friends had come to stand near them and listen as Uncle Joe talked to the paramedics, and Mr. Moseley stepped forward quickly.

"What happened to Eric?"

"He'll be fine. The Earnshaw boy ran his horse into Clover, and Eric fell off. Sprained his wrist, but he's not hurt badly."

"You telling me straight?" Mr. Moseley's eyes were intent on Uncle Joe's face.

"Yes, sir. He told me you'd be worried, but there's no need. Eric's tough."

"I need to get your p/r's," the veterinarian said apologetically.

"No problem." Uncle Joe swung out of the saddle and held Zorro's head while the vet put his hand on the black's neck, feeling his pulse and timing his respirations.

"Not bad. Pulse is eighty-eight. You'll have to rest him a few minutes until it drops."

"We'll be waiting for the Moseleys anyway," Uncle Joe said. "They stayed with the injured boy and his father."

Kayla came and took Icicle's reins from Sarah. "Why don't you go get a soda and sit for a while?"

"Thanks," said Sarah.

"Let's not unsaddle," said Uncle Joe. "We don't want to lose time when Becky and Eric get here."

"You think Eric can continue?" Mr. Moseley asked.

"I'll be surprised if he doesn't insist on it," Uncle Joe told him. "They're getting a rest now too."

"So what exactly happened?" Junior asked, watching the ambulance bump over the trail, back toward the stream.

"I guess that fool boy, Justin, thought he'd pass us while we were watering the horses." Uncle Joe shook his head. "He came tearing down the incline and ran over Eric."

"But Eric is really all right?" Miss Rose asked anxiously.

Uncle Joe shrugged. "Hurt his wrist, but I don't think it's broken. He landed kind of hard, but he was up and walking before we left."

"How about Becky?" Mr. Moseley asked.

"She's fine. I left her trying to keep Mr. Earnshaw calm."

"And the horses?"

"We'll have to look at Clover. She seemed okay, but I didn't have a chance to really check her over. The Earnshaw boy's horse was limping."

"He pulled a shoe," Sarah supplied.

"Is there a farrier here?" Uncle Joe looked around the clearing.

"The secretary said Sam's coming up here when he finishes shoeing a horse at the last checkpoint," Junior said. "The blacksmith from Sheep Mountain came up to help him, after all the horses got past the forty-mile point."

"How long have we been here?" Uncle Joe asked, looking at his watch.

"About twenty minutes, I think," Sarah said, and Junior nodded.

Uncle Joe took his hat off and wiped his forehead. "Becky and Eric ought to be here soon."

"Well, the paramedics are probably just getting there," Junior speculated. "Give them some time."

"Eric will want to take off as soon as they get there," Sarah predicted.

"Why don't you and Kayla see if you can get that vet to come check the horses again?" Uncle Joe ran his hand over Zorro's shoulder. "I think we're all set."

Kayla gave Icicle into Junior's care, and the two girls went to where the vet was chatting with the ride secretary's wife.

"Excuse me, sir. My uncle wants to know if you'll check our horses again," Sarah said.

"Sure will." The vet walked with her toward the pickup.

"Good recovery," he pronounced a moment later. "These horses are in great shape."

"Thanks," Uncle Joe murmured.

"You can leave any time." The vet ambled away.

A pinto came trotting in, and Uncle Joe hurried to where the rider was dismounting.

"What's happening with the boy who was injured?" he asked.

"He looks bad," the woman told him. "I passed the ambulance just after I came up out of the stream bed."

"What about Mrs. Moseley and her son?"

"That would be seventeen and eighteen?" the woman asked.

"Yes, are they moving yet?"

"No, not when I was there. I asked if they needed help, and they said they'd sent for it. There wasn't really anything I could do. They were staying with the boy and his father, so I came on."

"Well, thanks." Uncle Joe began to pace.

Mr. Moseley came to walk beside him. "Becky would want you and Sarah to go on and finish."

Uncle Joe said nothing. He went to Zorro and stroked his withers, then turned abruptly and walked past the vet around the trees to where he could see farther down the trail. Sarah followed and stood beside him.

"Uncle Joe, we're going to wait, aren't we?" she asked timidly.

He nodded. "I'm thinking maybe I'll ride back there."

"Then I'll go with you."

Uncle Joe looked at her. "You could stay here with Junior and rest."

"I have to stay with you," Sarah reminded him. "I wouldn't mind."

"We're close to finishing."

"It doesn't matter," she said.

He sighed. "I could let Mr. Moseley take Zorro and go to meet them. He's worried."

"He doesn't ride that well."

Another lone rider was jogging toward them, throwing a little dust cloud up behind him. Uncle Joe walked out to meet him, and Sarah followed. It was the young man in the red shirt.

"How's the Earnshaw boy?" Uncle Joe called.

"Not so good. They were putting him in the ambulance when I came through, and he was hollering." The rider looked so tired, Sarah thought he might fall out of the saddle.

"How about Eric and Becky Moseley, numbers seventeen and eighteen?"

"I saw them," the young man replied. "They were helping the boy's father." His horse jogged on.

"Let's you and me pray," Uncle Joe said to Sarah.

"Sure." Sarah bowed her head, but before she could say anything, Uncle Joe's voice came, quiet but fervent. "Dear God, please let that boy be all right, and bring Becky and Eric in safe."

Sarah opened her eyes a little and peeked at him. Her uncle hadn't hesitated to pray this time. He was staring off down the back trail.

"That's Siska," he said softly.

Sarah stared. A dust cloud moved toward them.

"Sure enough." She could make out Aunt Becky on the bay gelding, and beside them jogged a riderless palomino. Close behind them came Eric on Clover, leading Justin's chestnut quarter horse, Bullet.

"Yes!" Sarah cried. "They made it!" She started running toward them.

"Take the palomino," Uncle Joe called.

Clover and Siska were jogging side by side now, the Earnshaws' horses on either side of them. Sarah took off her hat and waved it, and Aunt Becky waved back, clutching the extra set of lines. Eric was holding Clover's reins low with his bandaged right hand, and his left held the chestnut's reins. As the four horses came close, a bigger cloud of dust appeared, and Sarah saw that it was the ambulance, lumbering toward them.

Uncle Joe jumped forward, laughing, and seized the chestnut's bridle. "All right! We've got some determined riders here, for sure!"

Aunt Becky laughed.

"How you doing?" Uncle Joe asked her.

"We're fine. We stayed until they had Justin on the stretcher, then we hightailed out of there." She slowed Siska to a walk, and Sarah reached for the palomino's reins. She and Uncle Joe fell into step beside the horses.

"Well, Siska and Clover had a pretty good rest at the stream, I guess," Eric said. "We ought to be able to move right out again."

"How's the wrist?" Uncle Joe asked.

"The paramedic wrapped it, but he said we should have a doctor look at it. They think it's a sprain," Aunt Becky said.

"Does he need an x-ray?" Uncle Joe's concern was evident.

"No, I don't think so."

They approached the checkpoint, and Mr. Moseley and Kayla ran out to meet them. Aunt Becky tossed her reins to Uncle Joe and swung her right leg over the saddle horn. Sarah watched as Eric's father held out his arms, grinning, and Aunt Becky slid down into them.

Just for a moment, Sarah envied Eric. He still had his loving parents: a complete family. She looked up at Eric and tried to smile, but it warped into a grimace.

Eric shrugged and said, "They're always like that." He hopped down and stood beside her.

Kayla came to take Siska's reins from Uncle Joe and led the horse toward the veterinarian.

"Everything all right?" Mr. Moseley asked.

"As well as can be expected," Aunt Becky said. "The chestnut lost a shoe back there, but I think he's all right. The vet should check his feet though."

The ambulance rolled slowly into the gate area, and the ride secretary climbed out of the cab. The driver waved and put the vehicle in gear, driving onto the gravel access road that came in to the checkpoint from the highway. The ambulance moved away in a swirling haze of dust.

Everyone at the checkpoint gathered around the secretary expectantly.

"They're taking him and his father to Baker. Looks like a nasty leg fracture, and maybe a concussion."

The vet was taking vital signs on the Moseleys' horses.

"You're all set," he said to Aunt Becky. "No need to wait."

"Great. I assume the officials will take care of the Earnshaws' mounts?"

"Yes, I'll check them over first," said the veterinarian.

The ride secretary approached her. "Mrs. Moseley?"

"Yes."

"In the ambulance, Mr. Earnshaw asked me to tell you how much he appreciates your assistance. We'll make arrangements to board the horses for them tonight in Brogan, and he'll pick them up tomorrow."

"Good," Aunt Becky said with satisfaction. She looked at Uncle Joe. "You hombres ready to do ten more miles?"

"Don't you want to eat something?" Miss Rose asked.

"No, I want to get this thing over with," Aunt Becky said. "How about you, Eric?"

"Are there any more cookies?"

The four mounted, and Rose handed Eric two cookies just as they clocked out, heading east toward Brogan and the finish line.

"This has been quite a day," Aunt Becky said to Uncle Joe. Their horses trotted side by side, despite their difference in height.

"It sure has."

"I asked Mr. Earnshaw if he'd mind if we prayed," she confided.

"What did he say?"

"He said, *Please do. I think we need it.* So Eric and I prayed for them."

"Justin was in a lot of pain," Uncle Joe reflected.

"Yes. I don't think he knew half of what was going on. That was the longest half hour of my life."

Eric looked over his shoulder. "He just wouldn't quit screaming, Uncle Joe. It was pretty nerve-wracking."

"One of those first two riders that came through had some aspirin," Aunt Becky said. "Justin's father gave him three, but I don't think it touched the pain."

"He didn't pass out when they moved him?" Uncle Joe asked.

"No. It might have been better if he had. But the paramedics said they would start an IV in the ambulance. I think they're giving him some painkillers."

They trotted on in silence. The sun was sinking behind them.

"We might have another hour or so of daylight," Uncle Joe said. It was after seven o'clock. "Barring any more surprises, I think we'll make it in pretty good time."

"Let's just take it slow and steady," Aunt Becky said.

"Agreed."

They jogged in to the final gate at 8:30. Rose, Junior, Kayla, and Mr. Moseley ran toward them cheering. There were fifty or more spectators, clapping as the riders crossed the finish line. Sarah recognized a few of the riders that had passed them, waiting for their final vet checks.

"What's the word on the Earnshaw boy?" Uncle Joe asked.

"He's at the hospital and going to have surgery on his leg," Junior replied.

"Your horses are looking good," the vet proclaimed. It was the same vet who had checked them at Crazy Springs that morning. "Ten minute recovery check."

"We'll be here," Uncle Joe said.

"You're just out of the top ten, I'm afraid," said the secretary of the final checkpoint.

"That's okay," Aunt Becky smiled.

"We won," Eric agreed.

"Feeling pretty chipper now, aren't you?" asked Mr. Moseley.

"Yeah, I feel good, Dad," Eric told him. "I could sleep for a week, and my wrist hurts, but I feel good."

"How about you, Sarah?" Junior asked.

She grinned at him. "It's a great feeling, Mr. Tate."

"Almost wish Joe had let me ride with you."

"You offered?" Sarah was startled.

"I told him if he was too busy, I'd take a shot at it. Didn't know as he'd want to get into this. You know, Joe's not much for competition."

"I know."

"Well, he's a good friend. If you need something, he'll give you the shirt off his back." Junior slapped her on the back, and Sarah groaned.

"You've got it pretty good, kid."

"Yes, I do." She looked up and saw Kayla, holding Clover's lead line, eyeing her wistfully. "Kayla, if you're serious about endurance riding, I think we might be able to find someone to sponsor you, after all."

"No doubt," Junior replied. "I've been hearing it all day from Kayla. Maybe Rose and I will practice up, and we'll try one of those shorter rides next summer, if that sassy Appaloosa of Kayla's is in shape by then."

The horses passed the recovery check without a problem, and the riders collected their T-shirts, belt buckles, and certificates.

"There's one more thing, Mr. Piper," the secretary said as he handed Uncle Joe his awards.

"What's that?"

"The top rider, Arnold Wentworth, asked me to give you this." He gave Uncle Joe a business card. "He said he was hoping to get a chance to talk to you all day, but he pulled out about twenty minutes ago. He's got some business for you, I think. Wants a good trainer to take his daughter's distance horse over the winter and keep it in shape while she's away at school."

Uncle Joe frowned at the card. "Wentworth, Wentworth. Might of met him over to Bend one time."

"His daughter came in fourth," the secretary said. "It's a good horse."

"Thanks."

"What's our official time?" Aunt Becky asked.

"Hmm . . . yours is fourteen hours, six minutes. Same for your son. Not bad at all. Joe and Sarah Piper clock fourteen hours, five minutes."

"Pretty impressive," Miss Rose said.

"This calls for a celebration," Junior agreed. "Where's the nearest burger joint?"

"I don't know," said the secretary. "Boise, maybe?"

"Well, I'm not going to Boise tonight," Uncle Joe declared. "Let's load these critters up and head for Elk Creek. If you see any golden arches on the way, pull over."

21

Sarah couldn't sleep, although it was very, very late. She kept going over the trail in her mind, one hundred miles of rough and smooth terrain, delectable and excruciating moments. And in between, lots of sagebrush and determination.

The low murmur of Uncle Joe's voice reached her through the screen. She got up and tiptoed to the window determined to close it, even though it meant shutting out the welcome breeze.

"It seems to me you have a very good life out here," Aunt Becky was saying. "I think Sarah will be happy here with you."

"I hope so." Uncle Joe's voice was low, and Sarah could barely catch his words. "I didn't know what I was getting myself into, but she's a good kid."

"You didn't expect to get into endurance riding, did you?" Mr. Moseley asked.

Uncle Joe laughed. "No, but it's not a bad pastime for a girl."

"There are a lot worse things she could be getting into," Mr. Moseley agreed.

Sarah smiled to herself. She supposed she could cover her head with a pillow or something, so she could leave the window open and not hear them talking about her. She was happy because she felt Uncle Joe was happy, more contented than he'd been for a long time.

"Think you'll do it again?" Aunt Becky asked.

"I don't think there's much doubt about that. Until Sarah turns sixteen, I'll just have to keep in shape."

There was a pause, and Sarah was already mentally reviewing the list of rides for the following spring. They could go to the fifty-miler in Boise! It wasn't far at all.

Uncle Joe said, "Can you folks stay over tomorrow and go to church with us?"

"I've got to be back at work Monday," Mr. Moseley said. "That means we have to leave tomorrow, and I'd rather not be driving after dark with the trailer."

"I s'pose." There was a deep silence.

"Eric's out cold," Aunt Becky said. "I think that pill they gave him at the hospital kicked in. We'd better get back to the hotel and get him to bed."

Sarah squinted in the twilight and made out Eric's inert form where he was sprawled on the grass beside his mother's chair. She felt sad, knowing her friends were leaving soon. It had felt so good, having them here. She wished they lived closer so she and Eric could ride together and study together, like they had in the old days.

"Do you think I ought to put her in school?" Uncle Joe was saying. "I've never been much of a scholar. I'd hate to have Sarah miss out on something important."

"She's bright," Aunt Becky said. "I think she's fairly independent in her studies now. Kids that age, if they're motivated, don't need as much structure and guidance as younger children."

"You think she's motivated?"

"Yes," Sarah breathed. "Say yes, Aunt Becky."

"She's sure motivated to ride horses," Mr. Moseley said, and his wife laughed.

CHAPTER TWENTY-ONE

"You could teach her a lot, Joe," she said.

"She's got the knack," Uncle Joe admitted. "She could be a good trainer."

"I think she'd study hard too, if you'd reward her for it."

"How do you mean?"

"Well, just staying home with you would be a big reward for her," Aunt Becky said.

"She doesn't want to be off at school all day," Mr. Moseley agreed. "She wants to be here with you and the horses. And she's always been a good student, hasn't she?"

"I don't know," Uncle Joe admitted.

"Well, I do," Aunt Becky said. "She's very good at math, and she loves to read. She's a good girl, Joe. Just give her plenty of books and give her a chance."

Mr. Moseley's voice came again. "Seriously, if you promised her something she really wanted—say, a colt to train next spring—I'll bet she'd break her neck to please you."

"That's not a bad idea," Uncle Joe said.

Sarah swallowed hard. She knew in that moment that Eric's father was right. She would do anything to please Uncle Joe, even without any rewards. But a colt to train, under Joe Piper's supervision . . . it was a delicious thought.

"It works with Eric," Aunt Becky went on. "This ride was what I promised him last year. He was dying to do a hundred-mile ride, so I told him last fall if he worked hard, we'd sign up with Laura and Sarah in the spring."

"I've been thinking I ought to get a computer," Uncle Joe said. Sarah caught her breath, it was so unexpected. "If I knew how to use it, I could keep track of my business better, I suppose. And then Sarah could e-mail her friends."

"She could teach you to use it," Aunt Becky assured him. "I seem to remember she's pretty good at things like that."

"You can get business programs," Mr. Moseley said. "Set up your finances on the computer and your schedule for training, all of that."

"What about chemistry and physics classes for Sarah, stuff like that?" Uncle Joe asked.

"Well, students can take just about any course online now," Aunt Becky said.

"You mean, by computer?"

"Yes. There are a lot of options for distance learning. Eric needs to take a lot of science, because he wants to be a vet, and he's taking classes that way."

"No kidding." Uncle Joe sounded impressed, Sarah thought. "Guess I need to look into that."

"It's not that expensive," Aunt Becky said.

"There's something . . ." Uncle Joe hesitated, then said, "I haven't mentioned it to Sarah, but I got a letter from Laura's parents last week. Sarah's grandparents, that is."

Sarah caught her breath and strained to hear every word now.

"Is there a problem?" Mr. Moseley asked.

"No, no. They just want to be sure she's doing all right."

"Why didn't you tell Sarah?" Aunt Becky asked.

"Well, the Andersons offered to pay for private schooling for Sarah."

"Private school?" Becky asked, and a chair creaked. "Is there a private school near here?"

"No. That's just it. They picked out a place near them, down in California."

"Boarding school?" Her voice rose in apprehension.

Sarah's jaw dropped. *No, no, no!* her mind screamed.

"You can't be serious," Mr. Moseley said. "Send Sarah away now to boarding school? She's just got settled here with you."

"Well, I'm not serious," Uncle Joe said, "but they are. They seem to think it would be better for her."

"No, Joe." Aunt Becky was adamant now, and Sarah gulped for air. Aunt Becky would stand up for her. "Sarah needs you. You're doing a wonderful thing, giving her a home here with you. Don't send her away. Please."

"That's what I was thinking," Uncle Joe said, "but I wasn't sure I was looking at it square on. I never raised a kid before, and I'm responsible for her education now. I love that girl, and . . . well, I don't want to send her off again, no matter how good the school is."

Sarah swallowed hard, feeling the familiar tears begin to burn her eyes again.

"We've got the school in Romney," Uncle Joe went on, "but I'm leaning toward just letting her go on the way she has been, learning at home. I think I just needed someone to tell me I was up to the job."

"You can do it," Mr. Moseley said. "If you need any support, give us a call."

"Yes," Aunt Becky agreed. "She needs her family right now, and a place where she knows she's wanted."

There was a moment of deep silence, then a shrill neigh and a loud thudding broke out in the barn.

"Goodness!" said Aunt Becky.

"That's that fool Buzz," Uncle Joe said. "Destructive on occasion. Likes to kick walls. I'd better go down there and check on things."

"We'd better get rolling," Mr. Moseley said, stretching as he stood up. "We'll be back bright and early for Siska." He went to Eric and prodded him. "Come on, buddy, wake up. You've got to get in the truck."

Eric moaned and sat up. His father helped pull him to his feet, and the Moseleys all climbed into their pickup. The engine started, the headlights came on, and the truck rolled out the driveway. Uncle

Joe stood watching them for a moment, then headed for the barn, and the lights in the barn came on.

Sarah made herself breathe slowly. *Thank you, Lord. Please help me not to disappoint Uncle Joe.*

She tiptoed back to her bed.

———————————

Siska nickered inside the trailer as Uncle Joe closed the tailgate, and Clover answered from the corral. Icicle trotted back and forth inside the fence, snorting.

"Guess they don't want their friend to leave either," Eric said.

Sarah stood silent, her eyes on Eric. His hair fell in a soft wave across his forehead, and she tried to memorize how he looked, all clean and fresh from a shower at the motel.

"I'll miss you all over again." The loss was already cutting deeply.

Aunt Becky came close and held her arms out to Sarah. "Be good," she said, hugging her close.

"I will, Aunt Becky. I'm really glad you could come."

"So am I. We'll call you often. We got a new telephone plan that lets you call as much as you want for one price."

Eric said, "Do you think Uncle Joe will go on more rides with us next year?"

"I think he's open to it," Sarah said.

Eric smiled. "I'll pray about it."

She gave him a quick hug. "Goodbye, friend."

"Bye."

Eric opened the passenger door of the truck and got in, rolling down the window. "Going to be hot again today." He moved over into the middle of the seat, and Aunt Becky climbed in beside him. His father was already in the driver's seat.

"So long, Sarah," Mr. Moseley said. "You help your uncle all you can, and come see us if you're out that way."

"Yes, sir."

Uncle Joe leaned down and looked into the cab. "Take care of that wrist, Eric."

"I will, Uncle Joe."

Sarah walked around the front of the truck and stood by Uncle Joe as Mr. Moseley started the engine. The family waved, and Sarah waved back. Uncle Joe just stood there, smiling a bit mournfully. Sarah wondered if it was even harder for Uncle Joe to see friends go than it was for her, since it was so hard for him to make them in the first place.

The truck began to roll, and Siska whinnied, loud and long. The eight horses in the corral answered and raced along the fence.

When the truck and trailer turned onto the road, Uncle Joe stirred. "Twenty minutes until we have to leave for Sunday school."

They hurried into the house and Sarah changed her clothes, then quickly washed up the breakfast dishes. Then she got her Bible and went back to the kitchen to wait.

Uncle Joe was ready on time, and they arrived at the church with five minutes to spare. Junior pulled in behind them and parked his gray truck beside Uncle Joe's pickup.

"Well, you old cayuse, where's your company?" Junior called, as he opened the driver's door.

"Gone and left us," Uncle Joe said.

"Oh, you poor thing." Junior laughed. "Must of been your cooking drove 'em off. I always knew you weren't much for cooking. Are you lonesome yet?"

"Powerful," said Uncle Joe.

Sarah smiled at their silly talk and their camaraderie.

"Sarah, maybe if you go out and bay at the moon tonight, Eric will come back," Junior suggested. "Are you going out on another hundred-mile jaunt next weekend?"

"No, but maybe in the spring."

"We'll see," said Uncle Joe.

"Eric wants to do the Tevis," Sarah said.

"Hm." Uncle Joe took his black hat off. "Full moon in July, huh? Possibility."

Sarah grinned. She could hardly wait until Eric called to tell her that he and his parents were home safe. He would go nuts when she told him Uncle Joe was thinking about taking them on the Tevis Ride.

"If you're going to make this a regular thing, I might have to try it," Junior said. "I 'spect Kayla will keep badgering me and Rose 'til we agree to take her."

"You'd have to do a sight of training if you expect your cow ponies to last through one of those rides," Uncle Joe said.

"Huh," said Junior. "That's all you know."

Sarah couldn't help thinking they sounded like Kayla and her little brother bickering.

They went into the church, and Junior went down the aisle to sit with Rose. She smiled up at him and moved over a little, adjusting her skirt.

"I really think she likes him," Sarah said, as she settled beside Uncle Joe in the next-to-last pew on the opposite side.

"So do I, but that doesn't mean they're thinking about marriage. Liking and committing are two different things."

She looked over at her uncle's handsome, sober face. "Do you think you'll ever be committed, Uncle Joe?"

He looked at her sideways. "I'm committed to you, kiddo. Don't you know that yet?"

Sarah smiled. "Yes, sir. I'm glad about that."

"Well, good. For a minute there, I thought you were talking about women."

Sarah settled back in the pew. "It's all right, Uncle Joe. You and I can get along just fine, just the two of us. For a while anyway."

He nodded. "That's right. I see a whole lot of horses in our future at the Piper Ranch."

"We'll be too busy for romance," she said.

"Yes, and we might have to expand our barn to hold them all. I'll need you to help me with the training. That's all we need to worry about right now."

Sarah smiled and patted his sleeve. "Suits me, Uncle Joe."